Does Harry Dream of Electric Sheep?

An adult social satire by John Altson

Illustrated by Kelly Morgan

ISBN: 9781502839978

Section I: The Voyage to Baa

Chapter 1: Memoirs

Please allow me to introduce myself. My name is Harry Enlightenment, and, by profession, I am a healer. I'm delighted that I have this opportunity to dictate my memoirs, as I have had, by any standard, a most interesting life.

Where to begin? In the beginning, I suppose...

I was the firstborn child of two Eurasian physicians. My original surname was "Brusselton", but I went through the necessary legal processes to change it to "Enlightenment" because it better suited my profession.

My education was almost completely accomplished online. I received a medical degree and then went on to get a doctorate in psychology and a second doctorate in divinity.

I had a highly successful healing practice in Amsterdam. My methodology was fairly simple and straightforward: I would listen carefully to what my patients would say about themselves, and then regurgitate that same information back to them. I'd say, "What do you think?" when asked any question. I'd ask them to pray for solutions to their problems and pray with them. I would make them feel good about themselves. Really, there was no magic involved. Most everyone left my practice better off than when they started their therapy.

Most of my patients were Earthlings but, over time, I administered to more and more aliens. Most of my alien patients were here on immigration visas, although some had arrived illegally. The alien patients were diverse and presented fascinating challenges. I should add that I would not administer to any alien who did not communicate in English — it was challenging enough to deal with their cultural heritages!

All of my alien patients were from our galaxy. Some came from Grappa, some from Cerebus, and a few from Ziggy. They were all disenchanted with their planet homes and looking for a better life here on Earth.

Healing the aliens was difficult, as their psyches were all quite different than the human psyche. Without exception, they had no understanding of an afterlife and no "faith" in a higher power. The healing process, for each of them, was one of mapping their psyche to the human psyche and then applying tried and true psychological methodologies. This usually helped immeasurably, although my "faith-healing" components were rarely successful.

The more I became involved with aliens, the more I became fascinated by the idea of doing what no man had yet done: travel to one of the remote planets, learn their culture, and then set up a healing practice on their own turf, as it were.

After a number of conversations with our government, I convinced them that it would be worth their while to allow me to travel on the next Galactic Shuttle. My argument was simple: I would act as an ambassador to inhabitants of a not yet contacted star system and convince them to become trade partners. Labor on Earth had become far too expensive and we were always in search of less costly labor sources on other planets.

The constellation Cetus has three planets, one of which (named "Cetus-2") was known to have intelligent inhabitants. One of our spy satellites, while hovering over Cetus-2, determined that there was intelligent "chatter" emanating on the surface below. I was very excited when I learned that the shuttle would drop me off on Cetus-2, where no Earthling had ever been. My grand adventure would soon begin!

Chapter 2: Arrival on Cetus-2

I boarded the shuttle on 6.7.3034 at 7:00 AM. I was one of three passengers. Sitting next to me was a distinguished looking gentleman, Pedro, who was a coffee sales executive from Greater Guatemala. Sitting across the aisle was a female Grappan, returning home to visit her grandchildren. As Earth quickly faded out of sight, we engaged in some idle chitchat before Dolly, our hostess, and a well-endowed Celeban, ushered us into our cryogenic pods, locking us in for our long sleep.

I don't remember dreaming while frozen in my pod. When I was awakened by Dolly, I remember her asking if I wanted some hot coffee to warm me up. I'm not normally a coffee drinker, but after a long cryo-nap, it really hit the spot; I could feel the warmth flowing from my mouth, through my body, and into my legs and toes. Needless to say, I was quite stiff after been frozen for a very long time (I had no idea how long). I got up and walked around, peering out of the windows as we approached Cetus-2.

Cetus-2 is a planet belonging to Durre Menthor, a sun-like star in the Cetus constellation; the ancients knew it as Tau Ceti. I was fascinated as we viewed Durre Menthor aglow a bright pale-yellow out of the port window while, on the starboard window, we could see Cetus-2, covered with a thick layer of rust-colored clouds.

I became increasingly apprehensive and anxious as we broke through the layer of clouds and into the atmosphere of Cetus-2. Had I made a wise decision? Would the inhabitants be hostile? I did not bring a weapon of any kind, as I am a pacifist by nature and all forms of guns were forbidden in Eurasia after years of debate.

The view of Cetus-2's surface was not unlike that of our dear planet Earth. There were landmasses sandwiched between two enormous blue oceans. There were pieces of land mirroring patchwork quilts, showing square patterns of shades of green. Obviously, the inhabitants had some form of agriculture. It seemed best that I should land my Planetary Landing Module (PLM) on one of the patches presumed to be farms.

Dolly laughed heartily as I struggled to get into my landing suit. I had been told that the planet's atmosphere was similar to Earth's, albeit with a little more oxygen and a little less carbon dioxide. I could easily breathe without being encumbered by any external device. Additionally, I was advised that the gravitational pull was less than the Earth's and that I could hop around with ease if I chose to do so.

My landing suit was computerized and was fitted with the latest technology. The spy satellite had monitored and recorded the "conversations" on the Cetus-2's "airwaves" and, through the recordings, had done a decent job of determining their languages, even including some of their idiomatic expressions. My landing suit's computer would automatically interpret their language in near-real-time and provide me with near-real-time translations. Surprisingly enough, it could map some of their language to English Language idioms! It had sufficient memory to record all of my conversations with the inhabitants and, luckily, those conversations were successfully captured and will be included in my memoirs.

I forgot to mention that both the PLM and my landing suit were equipped with speakers to broadcast my voice, translated into the alien tongues. Naturally, I needed to be sure that I pressed the button for the correct language output.

I was pretty well all set now. Dolly helped me into the PLM. It was fairly cramped with just enough room for my backpack, my briefcase and me.

The shuttle's executive officer determined that a particular plot of land would provide a suitable landing spot, so she set the coordinates on the PLM's computer and I was ready to go.

It took about ten minutes to cruise down from the shuttle and land in the middle of a grassy field. I knew that the Cetus-2 inhabitants spoke different languages, so I set the speakers on the loudest setting and turned on the pre-recorded message. It would play sequentially, over and over again, in each of the three dominant languages:

"Hello. I am a visitor from a distant planet. I come in peace and have no weapons. My purpose in visiting you is to discuss trade relationships with my home planet. I will not disembark until one of you approaches my spacecraft and offers to meet with me. I shall wait patiently until one of you chooses to come forth. Again, I am your friend and I come in peace."

I wondered what form of intelligent creature would venture forth to meet me. Would they believe my broadcast message? Would they send an army with weapons? I was very much at their mercy and, admittedly, quite frightened.

After what seemed like an eternity (but probably five or six hours), I watched as a creature ambled over from a point far off on the horizon. My first "close encounter" was just minutes away!

Chapter 3: First Encounter

My visitor approached cautiously. I laughed quietly as I observed that it was a biped sheep-like creature. It had two arms and two legs and seemed to be holding some form of weapon in its prehensile fingers. The creature's wooly head was relatively small, compared to its fur-covered body. Its rear end was large and disproportional. It wore no clothing.

As the creature came closer, I could see that its head was like the head of a sheep, with beady black eyes, a black shiny nose, and a mouth very much in the shape of a smile. Its two pink ears were erect as if standing at attention; the neck was a curious shade of red.

The creature spoke: "Come out slowly or I'll shoot!" came the first warning words. It seemed droll to see an erect walking sheep talking to me and threatening me with a weapon, but I heeded its advice and slowly opened the PLM's door, lowered the ramp, and descended. My landing suit's computer told me to use "Language #1" to address this creature, so I set the appropriate linguistic control.

"I am most happy to meet you," I said carefully. "I bring a message of peace from my planet. What is your name?"

"Leroy," came the response. "Leroy 76.45.900324, but you may call me 'Leroy.'"

"My name is 'Harry', 'Harry Enlightenment'. My planet is a great distance away. We are social creatures in a highly industrialized society..."

"I'm sorry; Harry, but I don't understand you. What does 'industrialized' mean?"

"My mistake. We invent machines that perform many of our tasks, making it easier to maintain a fulfilling lifestyle."

"Oh. We have machines too. The Technobirds build them for us. My gun is such a machine, see?"

With that, Leroy pointed his "gun" at a nearby clump of grass and pulled the trigger. A laser-like beam shot from the gun and into the grassy clump, leaving it smoldering.

"Very impressive! Do all of you have such weapons?"

"No. All of the '45s' do. Many other sects have guns. We need them to protect ourselves and our laws permit the use of any weapon."

"Interesting. Who are the enemies from whom you need protection?"

"They could come from anywhere. Maybe aliens like you with harmful intent. We have had quite a few alien visitors already, and not all of them have been friendly. We are always on the lookout for alien subterfuge."

"And what is a '45', pray tell?"

"Ah, my surname is 76.45.900324. The '76' is my gene pool and the '45' is my sect or social status; '45' denotes Baaners with red necks. Oh, yes - the 900324 is my i.d. within the gene pool-sect hierarchy."

"You all call yourself 'Baaners' then?"

"Yes. Millions of years ago we grazed and walked on all four legs but, over time, we evolved into the Baaners we are today."

"Are there other intelligent life forms on your planet?"

"A few. We call our planet 'Baa' as a reminder of our heritage. We also have the 'Technobirds' who build devices to our specifications. And there are the giant 'Ohmys'; they live in the land of Corporus.

Why don't you walk with me? I'll introduce you to my family and we can celebrate your visit with a traditional 'Jabber Roast'."

"That sounds wonderful. Let me grab my backpack and briefcase and we'll go meet your family."

We walked slowly through the field, then onto a path that led to what seemed to be a wooden farmhouse in the distance. Although my first encounter had gone well, I had so many questions. Maybe Leroy's family would open up and provide some of the answers.

****

It seemed obvious, in casually observing Leroy's naked body, that he was the male of the Baaner species. When we arrived at the farmhouse, I was introduced to his female partner Sue Ann 76.45.900622 and their two sons, Jake and Billy. After the formal introductions, Leroy invited me to join him on a tour of the property.

Leroy pointed to a fenced-in pasture next to his farmhouse. There, to my horror, I saw several hundred ape-like creatures, walking on all fours. They had ape-like heads and large furry bodies. "Here is where we raise our jabbers", said Leroy proudly. "We raise them for food and sell their meat in our marketplace. All of our furniture is padded with jabberwool!"

Here was my first major dilemma. I did not want to insult Leroy and his family by refusing to eat jabber meat, but I felt quite queasy knowing that I'd soon be eating one of my relatives. I tried to defuse the problem. "These are impressive animals, Leroy. I'm surprised that you eat meat, though. I thought that you'd live mainly on the plants that you grow here."

"We originally just ate plants, but, over time, we became both farmers and hunters. We try to eat a balanced diet of plants and farm-raised jabbers. Watch me as I select our dinner."

Without hesitation, Leroy aimed his gun at the head of one particularly fat jabber. He pulled his trigger and zapped the jabber, causing all of the other jabbers to scurry, making hideous howling noises as they scattered.

"Come; give me a hand, Harry. We'll drag this one over to my sons. They'll prepare the jabber for our feast tonight."

Reluctantly, I walked with Leroy over to the now defunct jabber. We each grabbed an arm and a leg as we dragged it from the pasture over to the farmhouse. Leroy told his sons to ready our dinner.

Jake, the oldest, was outside with Billy when we brought over the dead jabber. They were playing some sort of game that looked like chess and after Billy made some kind of foolish move, Jake chided him with "Come on, Billy. Do you have brains in your head?"

I thought Jake's comment strange, so I asked Leroy privately what Jake had meant. I'll never forget his response: "We have some sensory nerves in our heads, but the real brains are in our hindquarters. We just evolved that way. Maybe the brains in our rears came about because of the large layer of fat protecting them. When you meet other Baaners, you can usually judge their intelligence by the size of the rear ends."

While we waited for Jake and Billy to dress and prepare the jabber, Leroy had me sit down on a comfortable brown chair, presumably padded with jabberwool. He asked me to have a drink with him and, being quite thirsty, I graciously accepted. Leroy said that his beverage was called "Haykick", as it was derived from fermented hay.

Haykick did have a strange pungent odor, but it did serve to quench my thirst. It was amber colored, with tiny bubbles and a head much like beer. I bolted down six glasses of Haykick and reeled clumsily from the alcohol content. Leroy, on the other hand, could certainly hold his liquor!

Sue Ann interrupted our drinking, as she brought out a platter of carved jabber meat. The meat looked a bit like strips of chicken; it was flavored with some form of onion and had a mint-like sauce on the side. The "vegetable" side dishes were varieties of steamed grasses. Back on Earth, I was always a "meat and potato" guy. Our meat came from mammals. These jabbers were mammals too, not humanoids, but portly ape-like things. Not too intelligent, a bit like our cows. I could insult this family by not eating it and miss out on a potential treat, so why not give it a try?

We sat down on comfortable chairs around a large oval table and ate with our fingers (I am calling their prehensile limbs "fingers" for the sake of simplicity). The jabber meat was really very tasty after all.

When dinner had concluded, I had another awkward moment, as I needed to urinate and move my bowels. I whispered quietly to Sue Ann, "May I please use your bathroom?" She did not understand, of course, so I had to point to my genital area.

Sue Ann laughed heartily. "Please go out in any of the pastures. I will join you, as communal defecation and urination are considered some of our social graces."

Sue Ann took me by the hand and led me outside and into a nearby pasture where she proceeded to urinate while I pulled down my pants and took care of my bodily functions.

I could not help but wonder what other strange cultural nuances lay ahead!

Chapter 4: Absorbing the Baaner Culture

I spent several days with Leroy and the family, engaging in some most interesting conversations.

This is what I learned from them so far:

Baaners never lie. The law binds them to tell the truth.

Their laws are never questioned. They are always obeyed and respected. Their legal system was developed eons ago by a bearded Baaner (their "Supreme Chieftain") as absolute law. These original laws came mysteriously, and in tablet form.

Their form of government is what we would call democratic. Each town has a representative speaking for the town's interests. The representatives all meet periodically in a city called "Pastureton".

All "sects" (Leroy and family are "45s") have different belief systems and behaviors.

I explained to Leroy that I was sent as an ambassador, to see if there might be any trade agreements possible between our planets. He understood somewhat but suggested that I discuss the matter with their local governmental representative. Leroy said that all such representatives were elected into the "01" sect and were recognizable by their long beards. Representatives were thusly called "Bigbeards" and their local representative was Clarence 76.01.000278. At my request, Leroy invited Clarence to dinner at his farm.

****

Clarence arrived on time for dinner and was greeted by Leroy and his family. Clarence was taller than Leroy, seemed older, and had a beard at least two feet long. He seemed most cordial, even enthusiastic, as he greeted me.

"Good evening, Harry. Leroy has told me so much about you. I am really looking forward to knowing you better and seeing what we can work out as arrangements between our planets. Perhaps our jabber meat could be frozen and exported to your planet?"

Thinking quickly, I responded. "I do not think so, Clarence. We are actually descendants of a similar species and I do not think there would be much of an appetite, so to speak, for jabber meat. Let us talk and get to know each other better. The opportunities for joint ventures should appear naturally, you would think."

We sat down to dinner as Sue Ann brought out another jabber meat feast — this time the meat was ground into patties, fried in some form of grease, and served with raw onions. Once again, Haykick was the beverage of choice for the adults.

I was anxious to learn more about the Baaners' governmental structure, so I started the conversation. "Tell me, Clarence, for how long are you the elected town representative? Is it a lifetime assignment?"

"Indeed not, I'm afraid. My term is just for one year."

As an aside, Baaners have units of time similar to those on Earth. The cycle around their sun is 402 of their "days" and their days are more like 22 hours. For the sake of simplicity in my writing my memoirs, I shall ignore the dissimilarities and use our Earthly terms. Anyway, I questioned Clarence's one-year term... "Do you not need to spend time convincing others that you are worthy of another term? We call this 'campaigning.'"

"Yes, Harry. I spend far too much of my time 'campaigning', as you call it. It is necessary in order to keep my position and to maintain a continuum of representation."

"Why not extend the terms to more than one year? It would seem to be more efficient."

"Didn't Leroy tell you about our laws? They were passed to us by our Supreme Chieftain many years ago and can never be changed, even if we had a majority of Baaners. They are absolute in nature."

"If you cannot change the laws, what then do you do with your time besides campaigning? Please forgive me for being so blunt."

"We debate the interpretation of the existing laws and the enforcement of those laws; there are always new circumstances. Your proposal for a trade agreement is a good example of changing circumstances."

"I see. Let me ask you about trade agreements among Baaners. Do you barter? Do you have a form of currency? How do you survive, Clarence, if you give up your farming interests and get into a government position?"

Clarence scratched his long beard. "We barter, and we have a form of currency called 'chips'. I earn my living by being paid 150,000 chips per elected term."

"Then who pays for your services? Does the town?"

"In my case, 60,000 chips are paid by the families of Leroy's town and the other 90,000 chips are paid by the Ohmys."

"What? Do the giants pay most of your way? What have they to do with the town?"

"The giants create products that we pay for with our chips. They are very important to us because they lessen the financial burden on the town's residents."

"But is it not a conflict of interests if you serve both the town and the Ohmys?"

"Not at all. It has been a close working relationship. The Ohmys always have the Baaners' best interests at heart."

This aspect of the conversation stunned me. Surely, there had to be problems lurking in this arrangement. I had to think about it...

Clarence broke our silence. "Listen, Harry. I have an idea. Why don't you come with me to Pastureton tomorrow? You can stay at my home; I have plenty of room. You really need to meet more of us to better understand our lives on Baa. I'll get you broad exposure through one of my Mouthie contacts..."

"You lost me. What is a 'Mouthie'?"

"A Mouthie is one in the '02' sect. A Mouthie is one who communicates the latest news to all of the Baaners. Mouthies are highly respected and everyone listens to them and heeds their advice. They are very influential!"

I bowed politely to Clarence as he left Leroy's home. I assured him that I'd be ready first thing in the morning.

Chapter 5: The Road to Pastureton

Clarence arrived early the next morning. He came in a weird-looking vehicle driven by a "33" chauffeur. Let me describe it to you... It was called a "Trigo", a silver-colored open vehicle with two seats in the front and three seats in the rear. There were three wheels under the seated area, one in front and two in the back. There was some form of engine in the rear, fueled by methane gas, I was told later.

I bowed reverently to Leroy and Sue Ann, thanking them profusely for their kindness and their hospitality. As I said my farewells to the children (dare I say "kids"?) I thought I spotted a tear in Sue Ann's eye. I assured them that I'd try to visit them again before my return home.

****

The roads on Baa were quite bumpy; actually, they were more like paths than roads. We passed many farms and, as we passed each and every farm, the farmhands would stop their work and wave. Clarence must be most popular, I thought to myself.

It was a long ride to Pastureton, consuming most of the day. This was to my liking, as I had much to learn from Clarence about the workings of their government. Following are excerpts of my recorded conversations:

"Please tell me about the Baaners that you govern. Are they all members of the '76' gene pool? Do you govern anyone else?"

"We govern only the '76-ers'. The Technobirds and the Ohmys have their own form of government. How about your kind? How do you govern?"

"We do not distinguish ourselves by gene pool coding. Our surnames are based on past history and morph fairly frequently. When we choose a mate (we call it 'marrying'), the female usually takes on the surname of the male."

"Does that imply that the male owns the female? Please excuse my saying this, but your naming system seems quite primitive. It's all very confusing, but please tell me about your form of government."

I thought quickly. "We have a representative government, similar to yours – I think. Our officials are elected but have longer terms. One major difference is that our elected officials have the ability to add, delete, or modify existing laws."

"That's anarchy, Harry! If you are able to change the laws, you remove any semblance of stability. Our laws were handed down by our Supreme Chieftain and are never to be questioned."

"I need to think about that, Clarence. May I ask you some more questions? The Baaners are grouped into sects — I understand that. I also understand that some sects are determined by physical characteristics and that you can move sometimes from one sect into another. That's very confusing! Please tell me about these sects. How many are there? What are the rules from moving from one sect to another?"

"This may take some time. Please bear with me, Harry.

There is a coding space for up to 99 sects. The '01' sect, as you know, is for Baaner government representatives. All representatives must be males, are nicknamed 'Bigbeards', and are easily recognized by their long beards. If we are not re-elected, we must immediately shave our beards. Any males in the '76' gene pool may become town representatives.

The '02' sect is for the Mouthies. The Mouthies may be male or female and they are usually recognizable by their large mouths. The Mouthies are responsible for all forms of Baaner communication and, because Baaners never lie, we always heed their messages and behave accordingly. One cannot easily become a Mouthie; you are born as one or need to have some form of surgery to extend the size of your mouth.

Then there are the '08s'. They stain their necks black and worship 'The Holies'. They believe in a higher power and a personal deity. Anyone can become a 'Blackneck', as they are called, but it takes a life of extraordinary commitment. Blacknecks do not permit themselves to mate and may either be male or female."

"Please let me stop and ask you some questions. I understand the Bigbeards and the Mouthies but tell me about the Holies. What are they? Do you believe in them? Do just the Blacknecks believe in them? How did the belief system first originate?"

"You've touched on a really controversial topic. Some Baaners believe in the Holies. Certainly, the Blacknecks, but also the '09' Lumens and quite a few others. The Lumens are Baaners who glow in the dark, presumably because of their faith. I'm sure you'll get to meet with some of the Lumens; there are many of them in Pastureton.

All of this started many years ago when the Supreme Chieftain handed down our laws. The Supreme Chieftain actually claimed to have seen the Holies and conversed with them. I have trouble believing this because I've seen nary a one. Those that believe in the Holies think of them as invisible Baaner-like spirits that coexist with us, move around with us, and guide us with their codes of ethics."

"Amazing! I'd love to ask detailed questions of the Blacknecks and the Lumens. I interrupted you, though, are there other sects that I'll get to know in Pastureton?"

"Yes, Harry. Just a few more. We have a sect of 'know-it-alls'. We call them the 'Knowbies'. They are the '11s' and all have extremely large hindquarters. They are very argumentative and always want to try to change the interpretation of our laws. You'll see many of them in Pastureton.

You've already met some members of the '45' sect. They are Baaners who stain their necks red. The '45s' are quirky, love guns, and drink a great deal of Haykick.

Finally, there are two less fortunate sects. The '33s' are born with tiny hindquarters and limited intelligence. The 33s are those who perform menial tasks for us. My chauffeur, for example, is a 33.

The saddest lot is the 51 sect. These Baaners are born with no arms and serve no useful purpose in our society. I feel very sorry for the 51s. I wish we could do more to help them."

I asked Clarence the obvious question: "What happens to the 51s? How do they care for themselves?"

Clarence paused a moment. "They are all homeless wanderers. Eventually, many of them starve to death. The Knowbies recently proposed declaring them dead when they are born, so that we could use some of the other laws to provide for their families. It is very sad.

There is another point, Harry. We believe in the 'survival of the fittest'. Those sects who are weak and unable to care for themselves will eventually perish. Would you defy the laws of nature?"

I was stunned and had no good response. I could only summarize. "I'm beginning to understand the segments of the Baaner society. You have a great deal of diversity. In truth, we have diversity within our society on Earth. You have Rednecks and Blacknecks and Lumens. You have Knowbies, 33s, and 51s. Are there any 'normal' Baaners?"

"Oops. I forgot the 0 sect. There are not very many of those but, yes, they exist and have some representation in our government."

My head was spinning. So much diversity. So many challenges. Perhaps there would be ample opportunity for me and my healing services.

Chapter 6: The House of Baaner Representatives

We arrived in Pastureton late that same night; let me describe the scene for you... Pastureton is a large town on the bank of a pristine river. There are many wooden shacks crisscrossing along paths that we might call "streets". Towering far above the rows of shacks is a massive domed, wooden structure that Clarence said was the seat of government.

We settled into Clarence's house, a large four "bedroom" structure near the dome and across from a very large treed field. The home was furnished elegantly, with jabbercloth rugs and wooden furniture upholstered with jabbercloth. I had a spacious room with a methane gas lamp. Clarence lived alone with his chauffeur (who was also his butler). He told me that this was his Pastureton home and that his mate and two teenage daughters lived in their home back in Leroy's area.

Clarence said that I should get a good night's sleep because the next day I would sit next to him as an honored guest when the House convened for its daily meetings.

* * * * * * * * * *

Tomorrow came, and I have to admit that I did not sleep well; I was nervous and excited about my appearance in the House. Clarence and I walked along the path to the building with the great dome and entered through a magnificent arched doorway and into an enormous semi-circular room in which several hundred Baaners were seated. All of the eyes were immediately focused on Clarence, and of course on me.

The meetings were called to order after a salutation to their flag (a massive jabbercloth portrait of the Supreme Chieftain).

I should mention that the seating arrangement tended to group Baaners in the same or related sects. The Rednecks were together, seated with most of the Lumens. At the other end of the semicircle were seated the Knowbies - I knew them immediately because of their enormous posteriors. It was hard to pick out the 'normal' 0 sect Baaners. I'm quite sure they were those without red necks, without a luminescent quality, and without massive behinds.

At this point, I'll not subject you to all of the mundane chatter that took place initially. Rather, I'll discuss the topics that were debated in earnest, those of a particular cultural significance, such as the plight of the 51s. The House Speaker recognized Teddy, one of the Knowbies and the first to discuss programs for the 51s. Teddy spoke to the members of the House:

"My dear colleagues. The number of homeless 51s continues to climb; we have as many as two million of them in our midst. Watching them suffer and starve is unconscionable. We keep debating new assistance programs like the one I recently proposed, but they always seem to be voted down. I would like to propose that we take an informal vote today on Program 7181. The average Baaner tax increase would be only three percent and, with the new level of funding, we'd be able to refurbish our homeless shelters and improve our food distribution programs. It is our social responsibility to act now and prevent further misery."

Wally, evidently one of the more vocal Redneck Bigbeards, needed to chime in with his piece. "Misery, Schmisery. Shooting them is the best idea of all!"

The House Speaker (a Lumen) ignored Wally and politely responded: "We would like very much to provide better assistance to the 51s, but the economy is weak and further taxation would make it even weaker. I have always argued that taxes should be lowered so that more spending money is available to the Baaners. The Baaners would then buy more products, the Ohmys would receive more revenue, and they, in turn, would provide for the 51s. That should be the way our system works — the 'trickledown effect'.

It is also true that the 51s could be trained to become 33s, earn a wage, and support themselves and their families. Self-sufficiency is 'The Baaner Way.'"

The debate continued for at least one hour after which no vote was cast. I was interested in the role of the Ohmys in all of this. It seemed that they played an important financial role in the lives of the Baaners.

The next event, morning recess, caught me off guard. They did not have a "coffee break", but rather went outside, crossed the path, and entered the field across the way. Once there, they sang their national anthem, held hands, and had communal defecation. Maybe this was their way of bonding? Very strange!

****

After the morning recess, a debate started on the second topic: weapon control. I did not realize this, but quite frequently a young Baaner would go berserk and on a shooting spree, killing as many as several dozen innocent bystanders. Again, Speaker took the floor.

"Dear colleagues. Like all of you, last week's school shooting saddens me. As I understand, the perpetrator obtained his weapon legally, so there is really nothing we can do about it, other than making sure that the Mouthies discuss the negatives of random sheepicide. We cannot change our Second Amendment and the Ohmys producing our weapons would become angered by any manufacturing restrictions. We need Ohmy financial support."

Representative Teddy interrupted. "Dear Speaker. The weapon used was a military-grade rocket grenade. Surely we can encourage the Ohmys not to sell such weapons to ordinary Baaners?"

"Definitely not. The law clearly states that Baaners may obtain any weapon for their personal use and protection."

"But, Speaker, we have a culture of violence. Our entertainment media is permeated with unspeakable acts of violence. Can we not act to curb the negative influence of our media?"

"Here again, Representative Teddy, we cannot change the laws which permit absolute freedom of speech. We are bound to honor our laws."

And so, another heated debate persisted, ending in no resolution.

We took a luncheon break, after which The Speaker gave me the floor.

****

"My dear Baaners. I am honored to be here before you. As Representative Clarence has told you, I came to Baa as an ambassador, to explore with you the possibility of a commercial relationship with my planet Earth.

As I understand it, your technical know-how comes from the Technobirds, a group with whom I plan a later visit.

It is also my understanding that the product development, marketing, and distribution is done by the Ohmys, another group with whom I plan a visit. Am I correct in both assumptions?"

My response came quickly from the House Speaker: "Although you are correct in your assumptions, we do not advise that you visit the land of the Technobirds or the land of the Ohmys without a congressional escort. I'm sure Clarence would gladly volunteer to assist you."

"Thank you, Speaker. That is a fine suggestion.

We on Earth participate in what we call 'an intra-galactic economy'. If our partners on other planets can produce one of our commodities less expensively than we do, we attempt to negotiate a trade agreement. With a trade agreement in place, we then become the marketing, distribution, and customer service arms for the subject commodity. This form of partnership agreement has worked quite favorably for us and for our partners."

The Speaker then recognized Representative Jacob, one of the Knowbies, who proceeded with the first question: "We have considered such arrangements in the past, but they have always generated debate and discord. We are fearful that one consequence of such a trade agreement might be a rise in our unemployment figures. How can you guarantee that there would be no negative impact on our workforce?"

I replied. "There can be no such guarantee. We have wrestled with this issue ourselves. We arrived at two conclusions: (1) that these agreements comply with natural market forces and that breaking these forces is committing an unnatural act and (2) that the workforce can always be retrained for new challenges and opportunities."

This debate continued for another thirty minutes, after which Speaker concluded: "On the issue of the proposed intra-galactic trade agreement, let us review this together after your visits to the Technobirds and the Ohmys. In the interim, Congress will hold some internal closed-door sessions to debate the pros and cons.

You have not brought up the topic of immigration. I should remind you that my predecessor, Tramp.76.01.000977, was paranoid when it came to immigration. He actually misappropriated the government's funds to build a wall around Corporus, the island of the Ohmys. We all argued that the wall was unnecessary, as Corporus was an island. He did it anyway.

We are very protective of our workforce here on Baa. Who is to say that your planet might dispatch a large spacecraft to Baa and, under the cover of night, infiltrate our society with hundreds of illegal aliens?"

I chuckled to myself and then quipped: "Earthlings are so dissimilar to Baaners that we would quickly be spotted..."

"Yes", interrupted Speaker, "But how would we rid ourselves of your invaders? Would they politely express their sorrow for a misunderstanding and return home? You really need to give this more thought!"

I promised Speaker that I would do so. I lingered with Clarence for the rest of the day's congressional session, and then returned to his home to recapitulate and formulate my next steps.

Chapter 7: Watching the Baabaa show

As we walked back to Clarence's house, I observed him deep in thought. He finally spoke...

"You've seen our government at work, Harry. Were you disappointed in our inability to accomplish anything?"

I did not wish to break the law by lying, so I responded. "Yes, I was. It seems that all the House representatives do is debate and campaign. How do you get any issues resolved? How can you possibly govern that way?"

"We have our challenges Harry," said Clarence as he raised his eyebrows over his beady black eyes. "Sometimes we have to go to the Mouthies for help. If we win the support of the Mouthies, they can turn public opinion around and force resolution of any issue.

Having said that, I have a grand idea... I personally know the producer for Baabaa 76.02.001451. Let me give her a call. I think having an alien appear on Baabaa's News Hour would draw a large audience. We could use her show as a platform to get your views on some important issues and, at the same time, you could put out an appeal for a commercial agreement with your planet Earth..."

I cut Clarence short. "Brilliant! Absolutely brilliant! Let's do it as soon as possible. I did not see any media playback device in your home, though. How do the Mouthies communicate?"

"I guess I did not point out the Holovision projector in my living room ceiling. When I turn on the projector, three-dimensional images appear on my floor. They walk around and speak."

"We call them holograms. So, you have three-dimensional news commentators? I assume that you can only watch and listen?"

"Not so! The viewers can actually talk to the newscasters. Their comments are uploaded to the news studio for later analyses. You couldn't have quality media production without feedback, right?"

I was amazed. We had holograms back on Earth, but there was no way of offering feedback. I could not wait to see Baa's entertainment medium in Clarence's home.

****

We sat around drinking Haykick that evening and, after my goading, Clarence clicked a switch on his remote to activate the living room's projector.

"Watch this!" said Clarence proudly. "Baabaa's show is just starting. Please sit over here."

Clarence pointed out two seats at one end of the living room. We took our Haykicks over and sat down as the hologram image of a blonde-wooled Baaner slowly materialized in front of us. It was as if Baabaa was actually in the room! She introduced herself...

"Good evening, Baaners. We have the most interesting show tonight. My guests are two speakers, one a Lumen and one a Knowbie. Tonight, we are going to debate our healthcare laws. Let me first introduce Knowbie Harriet 76.11.008546."

Harriet materialized. She was a more elderly Baaner and needed a cane to help her to walk around. I could tell immediately that she was the Knowbie — it was apparent in seeing her enormous rear. Harriet took a position at Baabaa's left.

The Lumen guest appeared next and moved to Baabaa's right. Baabaa continued... "And now, let me introduce Mitch 76.09.007333. Welcome to both of you."

With Mitch in the room, I had my first close-at-hand look at a Lumen. Mitch had a small head that glowed a bright bronze color. He must have been a most holy Baaner!

"Let me fetch the first question. Here is a question from Lily 76.45.003549. 'I have a two-year old lambson who cannot get approved for healthcare coverage from our insurance carrier. He has a rare wool condition. What are we to do?' Harriet, you may take this one."

"Thank you Baabaa. We have a systemic problem with our healthcare system, and this is just another manifestation. Our law provides for healthcare insurance for all Baaners, but there is no guarantee that the insurance will cover all conditions! This pathetic little lamb will continue to suffer unless we take the Ohmy insurance corporations out of the loop. The government should process insurance claims, and that is the only fair way. The insurance companies are just out to make a profit."

Baabaa smiled coyly and then turned to Representative Mitch. "I know you have a response for this one, Mitch."

"Certainly, Baabaa. The Ohmys drive our economy and pay our salaries. It has always been that way, and they are entitled to make a profit in the insurance business. It's the Baaner way! And, after all, are not many of us shareholders in these Ohmy corporate entities? For the Ohmys, it's not about hurting the Baaners; they just make intelligent business decisions on what should be covered and what should not be covered."

Then came Baabaa's surprise. "I'd like now to introduce Lily and her two-year-old. They just happened to be in our audience..."

Lily stormed into the room carrying her lambson, sadly depleted of all of his wool and very, very pink. He was wrapped in a jabberwool blanket. "You just don't care!" she shouted. "Our government doesn't give a damn. What if this were your son?"

After Lily returned to her seat, there was a loud uproar in the audience and a chorus of plaintive "boos" interrupted the show. Baabaa regained control. "Our next question is from Zeke 76.45.004387. 'Why do I need to pay for healthcare insurance that my family and I don't need? We are all perfectly healthy and it's tough enough to just pay our monthly bills.' Mitch, how about it?"

"Zeke is absolutely correct. The whole concept of a universal healthcare system is totally flawed. I am of the opinion that any family should be able to 'opt-out' and each town should be able to devise their own healthcare system or choose to have none at all. It should be part of 'towns' rights'. Our government should not be telling each town what to do anyway!"

Baabaa knew that this would get an immediate response from Harriet. It did...

Harriet tapped her cane furiously. "No Mitch, no! Healthcare needs to be centralized and insurance remain mandatory. Who is to say that Zeke, tomorrow, might have a major health issue? Or his family? A governmental approach lends itself to economies of scale and making healthcare more affordable for everyone. We keep trying to dismantle the healthcare system when, in fact, the program is an approved entity."

There were more questions and the debate continued for the balance of the hour. We watched our holograms intently then after Clarence shut off the remote, I patted him on the back and said, "Please call her producer. I can't wait to get an audience."

I thought to myself that the Baaner audience would lift me to celebrity status and that I could easily have a lucrative healing practice here on Baa.

Chapter 8: Showtime

Karen, Baabaa's producer, jumped on the opportunity to have an exclusive interview with the first alien from Planet Earth. She told Clarence that she'd need time to put a panel together and that, during the interim, she would be sure that the network gave the coming interview sufficient publicity. Her plan was to recruit the panelists, put together a list of interview questions, and then give us a date. Clarence was happy to keep me as his guest until the show aired.

It just took two days for a response from The Baabaa News Hour. They had arranged to have media guests representing each of the "76 gene pool" sects: "Normal" Sect 0 Baaners, Bigbeards (Clarence), Blacknecks, Rednecks, Lumens, Knowbies, 33s and 51s. Each would pose questions from their vantage point within the Baaner society.

I thought the format was excellent and there would be ample opportunity for me to ingratiate myself with the viewers and put in a plug for my future healing services.

****

Did I forget to mention clothing? My goodness!

When I had first arrived on Baa, I was wearing my bright red spacesuit. The suit, as I had mentioned, was equipped with elaborate speakers and translation devices. Given this, how was I to mingle among the Baaners who wore not one stitch of clothing? Yet another dilemma.

Being truly resourceful and intelligent, I was able to use some of Clarence's tools to cobble together a headband that did the necessary translations and communications; it came with a computerized flip-down visor with which to translate the spoken words. Given this effort, I was now able to stroll about naked with the Baaners and join them in all of their social graces. It would indeed have been absurd to appear on Baabaa's show in my cumbersome spacesuit.

The day had finally arrived for the airing of Baabaa's News Hour. Clarence's chauffeur drove us to a massive building at the edge of one of the two great oceans. We were met at the front entrance by Baabaa's staff and herded, so to speak, to an enormous room with a circular stage in the center. Above the stage, and high in the air, were shiny sets of light sources that I assumed provided both the lighting and the image inputs for the holograms. It was most impressive, even by Earth standards.

We were escorted to our assigned spaces on the stage, after which Karen introduced us to each media panelist one by one. The first, Charlene, represented the "0" sect of normal Baaners; she was a young mother of three. Clarence, of course, represented the Bigbeards for sect "01". Following Charlene came Joseph, obviously a Blackneck; a male companion, not introduced, accompanied him. After Joseph, another Baaner ambled in. He was introduced as Timothy and, strangely enough, was with another un-introduced associate. Weird! Timothy gave off a soft amber light, so I knew that he must have been a Lumen.

The last four to step up to the stage were Billy Joe (obviously a Redneck), Betsy (very large rear end / Knowbie), Jeeves (Baabaa's personal butler and a "33"), and Michael (lacking arms and therefore a "51"). The stage was set for Baabaa's grand entrance.

And grand it was! Baabaa gracefully stepped onto the stage to a thunderous greeting. (I forgot to mention that Baaners do not clap their "hands"; they raise their voices and utter a loud bleat, kind of like "baah!")

Baabaa walked over to me and did a curtsy of sorts. "Welcome to Baa," she said warmly. "I trust that Karen has introduced you to all of our panelists?"

I bowed briefly. "Actually, Baabaa — may I call you Baabaa? The Baaners to the right of Joseph and to the left of Timothy have not been introduced to me. May I please know their names?"

Clarence looked puzzled as Baabaa responded. "Yes, you may call me Baabaa, everyone does. But Harry, there is no one there. Perhaps our lighting is too bright for your eyes and you have seen shadows?"

I was truly perplexed. There were two strangers: one standing next to Joseph and one next to Timothy. I did not wish to further embarrass myself, so I made my excuse... "You are right Baabaa. I am not used to such bright lights and I must have seen two shadows."

"No problem, Harry. As Clarence may have told you, this is my last scheduled show; I am retiring to my pasture tomorrow. It is indeed a pleasure to end my long career with an interview with our first visitor from Earth.

Before we start the show, I'd like to go over some minutia. Karen will give all of you a signal when the show is to start. After that, I'll greet our viewers and introduce you and all of our guest panelists. I will guide the discussions, question by question, being sure that all the Baaner sects are represented fairly. Most of all, the viewers will be interested in Harry's responses. There will be only two commercial breaks."

Everything went smoothly and according to plan. Baabaa gave me a delightful introduction and then proceeded to introduce each panelist. She then turned to me with a question.

"Before we get into our panelists' questions, I'd like to ask Harry to spend a few minutes discussing his planet Earth and his place within the Earthling society. If you don't mind, Harry?"

I was unprepared for this, but I quickly regained my composure and turned to Baabaa.

"It would be my pleasure, Baabaa. Our planet Earth is a member of the same galaxy. We call our galaxy 'The Milky Way'. Earth is slightly larger than Baa and has a similar atmosphere.

Our planet is over four billion years old. The first life forms, single cells, appeared over three billion years ago. The process of evolution then followed: Single celled animals became multiple celled organisms. These evolved into creatures of our oceans, called 'fish'. Our mammals, warm-blooded creatures such as you, came onto the scene just 200 million years ago. Whereas the equivalent of your species still thrives on Earth, it was the jabber-like animals that we call 'primates' which developed intelligence and became the dominant species. We call ourselves 'humans'.

Like you, we are social animals and have our unique socialization problems. That is why I'm so interested in the viewpoint of this panel, to see how you deal with similar issues.

Is that a sufficient overview, Baabaa?"

"Very good, Harry. You neglected to tell us your role on Earth, however."

"I'm sorry; please forgive me. I had extensive education on Earth, to prepare me for my role as a 'healer'. A 'healer' is one who deals with illnesses of the mind and of the intellect. He or she does this service for a fee. Surely you have such mental problems here on Baa?" I thusly planted my first seed.

Baabaa looked at me strangely and then responded. "This is a most unusual occupation, Harry. We do not have 'illnesses of the mind', as you put it. Our physical problems are handled by physicians and covered by our mandatory health insurance plan. There are no provisions for the conditions of the brain. Would you care to further comment on this, Betsy?"

Betsy, the Knowbie, turned to face me. She scratched her tiny wooly head thoughtfully. "This is largely true. We have personality differences that are always accepted as part of our diversification. It is further true that personality deviations from the norm are actually seen as blessings. Quite frequently, the 'abnormal' Baaners are those with creative genius. However, if any Baaner is mentally unfit and a danger to society, he or she is sent to Nowhereland."

I had always considered myself quick on my feet, so I turned to the panel. "Ah yes. I understand. Do you not have 'coaches'? Baaners who assist other Baaners in job transitions or in coping with life events?"

Baabaa answered this time. "Why yes, we have Baaners skilled in this type of service. We call them 'transitioners' because they help us navigate life's difficult transitions. They are highly educated and in short supply."

Yes! I thought to myself. There is actually an opportunity here on Baa. I had better mention the official reason for my coming though... "Thank you, Baabaa. I need also to mention that I am here as an ambassador, to explore the potential for trade agreements. I shall be scheduling visits to the Ohmys and the Technobirds."

Baabaa rubbed her "hands". "Let's get started then. Perhaps Clarence can ask the first question."

And so, we started.

"Do you have crime on your planet Earth? If so, what constitutes a crime and how are punishments administered?" asked Clarence. He walked over and looked directly at me.

I scratched my head to show deep thought. "I could go on for hours about this but let me try to summarize.

At the highest level, our definition of a crime is an act that is contrary to our legal codes or laws. Crimes, generally, can be against other humans or against property.

Crimes against humans include murder, assault, robbery, or rape. The punishment for these crimes varies from death to fines and / or imprisonment.

Crimes against property do not involve bodily harm and include robbery and arson.

There can be crimes against morality also. Prostitution, illegal drug use, and gambling fall into this category."

Clarence interrupted my soliloquy on crime. "We understand some of this, Harry, but you used some terms unfamiliar to us. I wrote them down. What is 'rape', for instance? What is 'prostitution'? What are 'illegal drugs'? Finally, what is 'gambling'?"

Improperly, I had assumed that these acts were common to all advanced cultures. I stumbled in my response. "Er, yes. Rape is the act of forcing one human to have sex with another. Prostitution is sex as a paid service."

Baabaa chimed in. "My goodness! These are strange crimes indeed. We have sex freely with one another and it is there is no payment for sex. This is most foreign to our thinking. If another Baaner wanted to have sex with me and I was not in the mood, I'd simply curtsy and walk away. Never a problem. Do tell us about drugs and gambling though."

"There are lists of products that are deemed illegal for consumption. These include mind-altering substances and improperly used medications.

Gambling is a term used to define the process of betting money in one way or another. Some forms of betting, however, are legal. Government lotteries are legal. Betting in a government-approved casino is also legal."

Baabaa was quick to throw in her opinion. "I like you, Harry, but you Earthlings are strange. We have no restrictions on our medications. If a Baaner wants to overeat a medicinal herb like weedacco, for instance, that's up to him or her. We're empowered to do as we wish. If there are consequences, so be it.

As for 'gambling', as you call it, we have no restrictions on how we play our games. Sometimes money is exchanged, sometimes not. Again, we are empowered to do as we wish. If a Baaner loses his or her money, it's his or her personal problem, and not a crime.

Clarence, would you kindly continue the topic and ask about punishment?"

"Indeed, Baabaa. Harry, you spoke of imprisonment and death as punishments. How are these punishments handed down? How does your legal system work?"

Trying to be a little more sensitive in my responses, I turned to face Clarence. "We have a system that we call 'judicial'. There are experts in the interpretation of the law called 'lawyers'. One lawyer represents the person charged with the crime while another represents the government. They present evidence, solicit witnesses and argue the case from both sides. When the debate concludes, a set of impartial humans called a 'jury' meets to determine if there is guilt or not. 'Not guilty' does not mean 'innocent'; it means that there was insufficient evidence to prove guilt. After the jury reaches their decision, a governmental employee called a 'judge' (also an expert on the law) decides the punishment, if any.

The death penalty is becoming increasingly rare. We eliminated the death penalty in most cases over one thousand years ago. More and more, our criminals are sent to prison for rehabilitation."

"Please excuse my ignorance Harry," spoke Clarence. "What is 'rehabilitation' and what is a 'prison'?"

"A prison is a government facility that provides food, shelter, and education to the criminal. The facilities and the staff are paid for by our taxes. Rehabilitation is the mind morphing that takes place in prison. Through discipline and education, we recondition the criminal mind."

"And does it work?" came Baabaa's questioning voice? "It seems to me that taxpayers are spending a great deal of money on a system with, perhaps, questionable results."

I was mentally exhausted already but felt the need to respond. "Actually, our penal system does not work very well at all. Our court system is backlogged with cases, and our jails are full. All of this costs the taxpayers dearly. I wish we had a better solution but back to you, Baabaa."

Baabaa took the helm again. "Harry told us, in a few words, about what he termed 'illegal drugs'. While the absence of laws speaks somewhat about our dealing with the use of medications, it is also true that there are differing opinions among Baaners. Timothy, we have not heard from you. What is your slant on misuse of medication?"

Timothy glowed even more brightly as he smiled and stated his position. "What we should have told Harry at the beginning of the show is that we have but ten major laws, the laws handed down by the Supreme Chieftain on his tablet. These laws are interpreted, case-by-case, by what Harry calls a 'judge' and sentences are administered accordingly. If one of our laws is clearly violated, the criminal is dismissed to 'Nowhereland', where he or she is left to survive, unsupervised, with other such criminals. The only taxpayer expense is the salary of the judge and the boat trip to Nowhereland.

Having said that, there is always an argument about the subjectivity of the judge. But, because we don't lie and don't question the law, the judge's interpretation of the law is the only potential problem.

Now, on those 'medications'. I personally am of the opinion that excessive use of any medication violates the law that states basically that our body does not belong to us, but to the Higher Power and that we are to treat our body like His."

As Timothy said this, the unnamed apparition next to him patted him on his rear in a congratulatory manner. Timothy went on... "If this is true, then ill-advised overuse of any substance is an attack on our body and in violation of a law, is it not?"

Betsy shook her massive behind in protest. "This is jabberwash, Timothy! How can any judge determine whether or not substance abuse has negatively affected the body? The question is far too complex. We are much better off leaving Baaners empowered and determining their own fates."

Baabaa jumped in immediately. "There you have it, Harry. See — there are always two sides to any story. Now that I've stirred the pot, let's go to two opposing views on crime. Billy Joe, let's hear from you now."

Billy Joe ruffled his red neck. "We Baaners have far too much crime. Homeless 51s are settling in our pastures. The 33s are stealing our valuables when we are not home. We need to ship all the 33s and 51s to Nowhereland and only that will solve the problem. I'm sure glad we all have our guns ready at home!"

Joseph, the Blackneck, moved to center stage as his unnamed apparition drifted behind him, whispering in his ear. "No, no, no! Banishment to Nowhereland is not the solution and neither are guns! We need to love one another and treat the needy with dignity. Should we not take the 51s and 33s into our homes, if they are facing difficulties and we can afford to do so? The answer here and always is love."

Without saying a word Jeeves, the 33, and Michael, the 51, smiled and pranced about. Joseph had struck a harmonious chord.

Baabaa loved the contention. After all, the more the discord, the better the viewer ratings, and she wanted high ratings for this, her last show. She moved right along. "Finally, on the broad topic of crime and punishment, let's discuss Harry's death penalty. Billy Joe?"

"You bet! Thanks, Baabaa. As Baabaa said earlier, our criminals are all sent to Nowhereland, regardless of their crime. It is a one-way ticket. The 'better' criminals band together and live as best they can in Nowhereland while the 'badder' criminals tend to be loners and survive in whatever way possible. While there are sheepicides and killings from time to time, we never stoop to the levels of the criminals and administer a sentence of death."

"Wait just a minute!" clamored Betsy as she again wiggled her rear. "What about the 'stand-your-ground' law and executions that come about as a consequence? Is that not an act of murder?"

Billy Joe jumped up and down. "If a baddie comes after my property or threatens me, I'm entitled to use my gun and shoot him down. That's the law from our Supreme Chieftain. You cannot question his wisdom."

And so, Baabaa prevailed in her calming voice: "There, there now. Let's not get too ruffled. We have many more questions to ask about Harry."

And so, I grimaced. What would they think of next?

****

"One of our viewers would like to know if you have wars on your planet," said Baabaa. "Do you humans live peacefully or is there some form of armed conflict?"

"For as long as humans have been on Earth there have been battles and wars. Our government has a large defense budget to assist us in the event of war. The defense budget pays for soldiers and advanced weaponry. Having sophisticated weapons and a large army actually acts as a deterrent, preventing unwelcome aggression and acts of terrorism.

I should mention also that our government acts as a police force for the planet. If there is strife anywhere, we send in our soldiers to bring about a peaceful resolution. It's really not too complicated."

The panel listened carefully. Without exception, they all seemed aghast and surprised. Baabaa broke the silence. "But it is complicated, Harry. We Baaners never have major strife of any form. We do, however, have a defense budget to fund an army and weapons to protect us in the event of an alien invasion. The Ohmys insist on having a strong defense. Clarence, I see your arm raised..."

"Thank you, Baabaa. While you came by yourself and in peace, Harry, there is no doubt that other aliens may attack Baa and pillage our property. We must be prepared for that eventuality and have a well-trained army. In addition, we are always improving our weapon systems with technology from the Technobirds and Ohmys. The one fundamental difference between Baaners and Earthlings seems to be your concept of a police force to combat strife around your planet. It seems to me that your government would be better off not having the expense of a police force and letting Earthlings settle their own disputes."

As I mulled over Clarence's comments, Betsy took the floor again. "Clarence, you know my position on this. My cynical view is that we fund a defense budget only because the Ohmys want employment in their factories. We have never had an alien invasion and we probably never will. The Ohmys, and perhaps our government, want to keep us Baaners in a state of fear so that we focus on bogeymen coming from other planets and not on our dysfunctional government!"

Clarence stomped his hoofs. "I take offense at your accusations, Betsy. Who is to say that a band of terrorists might land on our planet tomorrow with the sole purpose of annihilating our crops? Further, you ignore the fact that many of our young Baaners find career employment in our army. Harry, is your army comprised of paid soldiers also? It is an honor to serve in our Baaner Army."

I thought about the historical implications of Clarence's question. "We used to have a system of mandatory army service but, over time and with our poor employment percentages, it became much more desirable to join our troops as a paid volunteer. We now have a well-paid and well-trained defense force."

Baabaa looked over at the clock on the wall. "Interesting debate, panelists. Let's take a short commercial break."

We all walked over to an urn that contained warm grasswater. I grabbed a cup and walked over to Clarence. "This is a tough group. Is there always this level of dissension?"

"Yes, my friend. Just wait until the other speakers start in!"

This gave me a good idea. During the commercial breaks, I would introduce myself to each of the media moguls and, perhaps, get to meet them individually. There is nothing like a candid one-on-one discussion!

I excused myself from Clarence and walked over to Betsy.

"Good evening, Betsy. I was struck by your comments on the role of The Ohmys. I'd very much like to discuss this and other topics with you over lunch. Might that be possible?"

Betsy smiled and bowed gracefully. "Absolutely, Harry. Here is my business card. I'm on vacation next week, so why don't you have Clarence take you over to my home. You may stay for a few days and we'll get to know each other better. I'm sure we can learn a great deal from each other."

Wonderful! I could not have planned this any better. Let the show go on...

****

"Welcome back!" exclaimed Baabaa as she continued after the break. "We have had a lively discussion already, having heard from the Bigbeards, the Blacknecks, Rednecks, and Knowbies. Let us give the '0' sect a chance now. Charlene, do you have a question for Harry?"

"Hello everyone. My name is Charlene 76.00.035688 and I am honored to be on Baabaa's show. My mate and I own a small pasture just outside of Pastureton. We have a happy but simple life living off of the land and selling our produce in the marketplace.

I have but one question for Harry. Let me try and frame it properly. Although we have just ten basic laws, the interpretation of those laws has caused great divisions among the Baaners. We have Bigbeards, Rednecks, Lumens, and Knowbies. They all have differing opinions and those differences have resulted in a polarized society and a paralyzed government. It seems that nothing gets done in Pastureton. Harry, tell me — Do you have such divisions on Earth?"

"We do, Charlene. It is a necessary consequence of democracy and freedom of speech. If you have a dictator, then everyone flocks to abide by his opinions; there is no other option. In a 'free society' such as your society and such as mine, you have natural divisions that evolve over time."

"But tell me then; do you have humans that do not take extreme positions on everything? Normal beings, like my mate and my children?"

"We used to have Earthlings that referred to themselves as 'The Silent Majority', but they diminished in number over time. Now you have to take a side on one extreme or another."

Charlene then did the unexpected. Angrily, she turned to Baabaa and shouted, "It's your entire fault! The media creates divisions by stirring up controversy. You thrive on discord. Your ratings would suffer without discord. Admit it, Baabaa!"

Though sheepishly, Baabaa maintained her dignity. "There is some element of truth to your accusations, Charlene. We need our ratings to maintain advertising revenues. But, as we've pointed out repeatedly on this show, Baaners pride themselves on freedom of speech. Should we not elicit viewpoints from every extreme to educate our viewers? Let's go to the next question. Joseph?"

Blackneck Joseph walked to center stage, his shadowy apparition-like associate trailing along next to him. I was able to see Joseph's friend more clearly now. He was Baaner-like but almost translucent; he was unlike any that I'd met previously. Joseph bowed gently and addressed me. "As you know, Harry, we Blacknecks dedicate our lives to the service of our Higher Power. It is our duty, therefore, to instill some semblance of faith among all Baaners. We believe in an afterlife and that, to partake in the joys of that afterlife, we must believe in The Higher Power and abide by the laws passed from Him to our Supreme Chieftain. Does this make sense to you? Do Earthlings believe in a higher power? Do they believe in an afterlife?"

I thought this an easier question, as I was a person of faith, had a doctorate in divinity and considered faith healing in my practices. "Yes, Joseph. We have sects as you Baaners do, although they are less formal and less well defined. Most humans have some form of faith and most believe in an afterlife. It varies very much by 'sect'. Many of us believe that the fundamentals of our codes of ethics were passed down as a tablet from our higher power."

Joseph's silent companion whispered in his ear and Joseph came over next to me. "This is worthy of a lengthy discussion and one not suited for this audience. Here is my card, Harry. Please contact me after the show."

There were grumbles in the audience which Baabaa quickly dispelled as she gave the signal for the next commercial break.

What did Baabaa have up her sleeve, so to speak, for the grand conclusion of the show? "Time will tell." I thought to myself.

****

The audience was on their feet after the commercial break. This was the last segment of Baabaa's last News Hour and they could not wait to give her a big sendoff after the next set of speakers.

Baabaa was all smiles, taking in all of the adulations. As the applause ended finally, she introduced the next panelists. "Thank you, thank you! Our next question comes from Jeeves, Clarence's chauffeur. Jeeves, if you would?"

"Thank you, Baabaa. Harry, we've gotten to know each other for a few days now, but I've never really had the chance to ask you any questions of any substance. Perhaps this is not the right forum, but here goes...

As you know, I am a '33' and a part of the Baaner proletariat/working class. My parents were hard-working 33s and I'm happy to have a job as Clarence's chauffeur; not all of us 33s are as fortunate. I am concerned about what will happen to me if Clarence is not re-elected, for instance. I live in a constant state of anxiety.

My questions to you are these: How do humans move upward from one sect to another? How do humans break out of the working-class rut? Are there education programs set up by your government?"

I dared not mention that I was the offspring of two well-to-do physicians, so I answered as truthfully as I could. "It is difficult on our planet also. Those Earthlings with means tend to provide quality education for their offspring. They also provide their children with the proper learning environment and the proper technological tools to develop their skills.

The middle class and poor are deprived of the proper tools for skills development and find it difficult to break out of their 'sect'. Yes, there are some government programs to help fund education, but they are limited due to budgetary constraints. One of our famous authors wrote a book called 'Animal Farm' in which he portrayed a society in which everyone was equal, but some were more equal than others. I wish I had better news for you."

"Well, then," continued Jeeves. "Do you suspect that your equivalent of our Ohmys might be playing a role in suppressing educational programs? That they might want a large pool of inexpensive labor always available?"

The audience sighed a collective gasp. Someone was actually questioning the integrity of the Ohmys! This question caught me off guard but, as always, I needed to provide an honest response. "I have no proof of this, Jeeves, but there are humans that may agree with you."

Baabaa, not wishing to anger her Ohmy sponsors, quickly thanked Jeeves for his contribution and went on to the next (and last) guest. "Our last guest panelist is one of our homeless '51s'. Welcome, Michael. We're running a tad late, but is there a short question you wish to ask of Harry?"

Arm-deprived Michael was visibly unhappy that his interview time was limited. His question was blunt. "Do you have a homeless population on Earth? Who are they and how are they cared for, if at all?"

I felt so sorry for Michael and I wanted to give him a most thoughtful answer. Maybe it did not come out right... "Unfortunately, we have our homeless too. They come from all of our sects, however. Some come from families already homeless, some are substance-abusers, some have diseases of the mind, and some do not wish employment of any sort. There are more and more of these unfortunates and we, like you, just don't have the budget to provide adequate food and shelter..."

As if on cue, Michael bolted to the entrance to the studio and butted the door open. Brushing aside all of the security guards, hordes of armless 51s came streaming into the room and onto the stage and creating an uproar in the audience.

"There!" said Michael boldly. "Here are a few of my friends. Baabaa, please give them a welcome."

Baabaa was visibly shaken. I'm sure she was thinking that this was not the way her last show should be ending and how could she turn a potential disaster into a winning PR move? Her response was both timely and brilliant.

"Welcome, all of you 51s! I am glad to have you as guests on my last show. We do not have time for proper introductions but I'm going to invite each of you to my home next week for a party in your honor. Each of you may bring your family and each of you will be given a brand-new Lamb-ergini Trigo to take home with you!"

The audience rose to their feet and provided five minutes of thunderous applause. Baabaa had pulled it off as far as the audience was concerned but, I thought to myself, what use was a Lamb-ergini to a Baaner with no arms? Oh well...

On the way back to Clarence's home, I thanked producer Karen for her efforts and requested the contact information for each of the panelists. Besides getting together with Betsy and Joseph, I wanted to be sure to get a better understanding of all of the other sects. How else could I prepare for a lucrative healing practice later on?

Chapter 9: My days with Betsy

Jeeves was kind enough to drive me over to Betsy's home. I said my 'goodbyes' to Clarence and Jeeves, and then walked up a long winding path to Betsy's front door.

Betsy had a magnificent home at the top of a steep hill. Wildflowers and exotic grasses surrounded the house and you easily could see Pastureton in the distance from her front porch. I knocked on her door.

"Hello, Harry. Please do come in. I've been looking forward to spending some time with you. I'm glad you survived Baabaa's show." She ushered me in, and we sat down in her spacious living room.

"Thank you. The Baabaa News Hour was more stressful than I anticipated. Have you known Baabaa for a long time?"

"We were actually roommates in college. She's quite a Baaner, don't you think? Let me pour you a cool drink."

Betsy ran off to the kitchen and returned with two tall glasses of Haykick. "There now. How do you like our lives on Baa? It must be a mind-opening experience."

"That's putting it mildly, Betsy. The funny thing is, there are many similarities between our cultures, more than you would expect. We have many of the same social mores, for instance. We have a similar form of government also. One big difference is that 'women', the female of our species, have an important role in our government. Our current 'president', or executive leader, is in fact female."

Betsy almost fell out of her chair in amazement. "How did you know that I wanted to discuss the rights of females with you? I have a meeting with some of Baa's most powerful ewes this evening and I was hoping that you'd join us as my guest. We will be discussing our rights as female Baaners."

"Count me in. I'm sure that I'll learn a great deal. I noticed that you refer to female Baaners as 'ewes'. Are there other terms I should know prior to tonight's meeting?"

"A few important things, Harry. Firstly, we ewes refer to ourselves as 'Eweish' and there are three classes of Eweish Baaners: orthodox, conservative, and reform. I am an orthodox ewe, which means, basically, that I follow long-standing dietary traditions and go to worship once a week. Conservative ewes have fewer rules by which to abide and reform ewes kind of do their own thing."

I was curious about what I might be eating while visiting Betsy, so I asked tactfully. "What dietary restrictions do you live by, Betsy? I do not wish to offend you while in your company."

Betsy laughed until her large rump bounced up and down. "No problem, Harry. Orthodox ewes only eat grasses; we are not carnivores. This custom started many years ago when jabber meat was considered unsafe to eat. Since then, the government has put strict meat inspection procedures in place and jabber meat probably is safe to consume. I remain loyal to our old customs, though. The meals I prepare for you will be comprised of grasses from my garden. I hope you're alright with this."

"Absolutely, Betsy. I have gotten used to the Baaner grasses. Some of them are quite tasty.

On our planet, we call humans who do not eat meat 'vegetarians'. They avoid meat mostly for health-related reasons."

"And are there different types of vegetarians?"

"You may be sorry that you asked! A 'flexitarian' is a human who will occasionally eat meat or animal products. A 'pescetarian' eats some seafood. An 'ovo-lacto vegetarian' will eat animal products limited to eggs and milk. A 'vegan' eats plant-based foods exclusively, while a 'raw vegan' will only eat raw vegetables. Then there are 'freegans' who socially eat meats only so as not to offend other humans. Finally, there are 'locavores' who eat only locally grown plants."

"Too much information!" laughed Betsy. "Considering all of those definitions, I guess I'm a 'vegan'. By the way, no Baaners ever eat seafood or fish. We are of the opinion that all seafood contains contaminants such as mercury. You will never see seafood in our stores or restaurants. We do not eat eggs and the only time we serve milk is to feed our children; we have no milk-related products. I suppose our diet is much, much simpler than yours. Mostly grasses."

I contemplated the next question carefully. "Some of us have become vegetarians for moral reasons. They think it cruel to kill animals for food. How do you feel about that?"

"I agree with them. Many of us also believe that jabbers have some form of intelligence and it would be barbarous to eat them or any other animal for that matter."

We chatted some more, and then strolled around her garden picking choice grasses for our evening meal. Betsy then drove over to the meeting in her Trigo.

****

Betsy was the guest speaker at the evening meeting of "Ewes United". She spoke passionately about the biases of the "01 sect" politicians / bigbeards. What I did not know was that the tablet passed down ages ago by the Supreme Chieftain spoke vaguely about the males/rams running the political structure for the government. It was like humans using the term "men" to mean both men and women. The Eweish interpretation of the tablet was that exactly, and Ewes United felt that the rams were actually less suited to run the government than the ewes. Ewes were allowed to vote but were never allowed to hold political office — they could not grow a beard!

Betsy introduced me to her audience, and I received a chorus of "baahs" as an ovation. I said that I understood their dilemma completely and that, many years ago, we humans had our "Women's Suffrage" movement to obtain the right to vote for females. I also explained our women held many positions of power within our government. All of this fired them up so much that, at the conclusion of the meeting, they actually agreed to plan a massive "March on Pastureton". Exciting times!

We rode home, shared a couple of Haykicks, and then settled in for the night.

****

I spent three days with Betsy. We toured the area in her Trigo, we had some memorable meals, and we talked incessantly about Baaner politics. I guess we would call Betsy "part of the liberal media", given her viewpoints.

The last meal prior to my getting together with Joseph the Blackneck was quite memorable. Betsy had put together a veritable banquet. Her dining room table was full of vases of flowers from her garden and she kept bringing out one sumptuous dish after another. Needless to say, we accompanied her meal with many glasses of cool Haykick.

The dinner conversation took an interesting turn. I don't know how it started, but we got on the subject of same-sex relationships. Here are snippets of my recorded conversation with Betsy:

"We have same-sex relationships on Earth. Some sects permit a formal, government sanctioned relationship (we call it 'marriage'), some sects informally condone such relationships, and some sects find it a violation of their laws."

Betsy had trouble absorbing this and pounded me with questions. "How can these relationships bear offspring? What are their lives like? How do they socialize? Is this not against your religions?" She was very curious.

"On the subject of offspring, in many cases, the same-sex couple will adopt an unwanted child. In other situations, a male-male pair will fertilize the egg of a host female as a financial transaction. In the female-female pairing situation, the females will sometimes choose a sperm donor from a 'sperm bank' and become pregnant with the sperm from an unknown donor."

Betsy almost fell on the floor. "Do you have any idea how this sounds to an alien culture? Adoption? Unwanted children? Host females? Sperm banks? Surely you are jesting!"

"Not so! Let's talk about religions. In my religion, for instance, it's all about love. If you truly love one another, it does not matter if that person is of the same sex or not. Relationships and even marriage should be solely about love.

You also asked about the lives and socialization of same-sex couples. In my 'sect', same-sex couples live together and socialize with other same-sex couples. In many cases, they also mix freely with opposite-sex ('heterosexual') couples. It is becoming more and more the norm to have a mix of same-sex couples and heterosexual couples."

Betsy smiled before launching the next question. "Do you then have sex with other species? Are there inter-species relationships or marriages? Would you like to have sex with me, Harry?" She batted her eyelashes.

I was caught completely off guard by this question. I went over to Betsy and gave her a big hug. "I think you are a most beautiful ewe, Betsy, but I'm afraid you're not my type. Please do not be offended."

Betsy laughed heartily. "I was just testing you, Harry! You're not my type either, but I like you a lot."

We ended the evening on that high note, and I prepared myself for tomorrow's meeting with Blackneck Joseph.

Chapter 10: Joseph and the Holies

My new friend Betsy was kind enough to drive me over to visit with Joseph. Joseph had told me earlier that he lived with twenty or so Blacknecks in a newly constructed building on the outskirts of Pastureton. Like our Roman Catholic priests on Earth, they all had made a lifelong commitment to the Holies and taken vows of poverty.

I rang the brass bell outside the front gate to alert Joseph of my arrival and, shortly thereafter, he strolled over from the main building. As was the case on the Baabaa's News Hour, his translucent companion was there with him. Bowing, Joseph opened the gate and warmly greeted me.

"It's so good to see you, Harry. Please do come in and meet my brothers. We have much to discuss. How have you been?"

I told Joseph that I was enjoying my stay on Baa and had taken copious notes while studying the Baanan culture. I asked him to please introduce me to his companion, but he looked strangely at me and, as was the case on Baabaa's show, I made excuses about seeing shadows. What was going on? How come I could see these apparitions but no Baaner was capable of seeing them? This was my biggest mystery thus far. So, ignoring his friend, we ambled into the front entrance of the main building.

"Come in, Harry. My brothers have been eagerly waiting for you. We've delayed our hour of prayer so that you could join us."

When we entered the main foyer, there was a large auditorium to the right. In that same auditorium were all of Joseph's fellow Blacknecks and each had his own apparition by his side! I dared not seem delusional, so I just simply ignored the "extras" and kneeled next to Joseph in prayer.

A Blackneck by the name of Josiah led us in prayer: "Dear brethren, we are gathered here in prayer today thankful for this opportunity to break bread with our Brother Harry from Planet Earth. In this prayerful session, we will quietly meditate and reach out to the Holies, so that they might guide us in our works. We thank you, dear Holies, for our good health and the wisdom that you impart. We pray, also, that Brother Harry may provide wisdom and guidance through his Earthly perspective."

The entire congregation of Blacknecks quietly kneeled and meditated. The ghostly apparitions stood next to them, some of them actually with their arms around the Blacknecks. As I kneeled beside Joseph, I wondered what wisdom I could possibly provide to these very holy creatures. Although I had a doctorate in divinity, I was not terribly religious back on Earth. What could I possibly say? I'd do my best, I guess.

It seemed like an eternity, but after an hour or so Brother Josiah ended the meditation session. Joseph beckoned me to walk with him in their herb gardens.

"Tell me, Harry, do you have Holies on your planet? What form of religion do Earthlings have?"

"I spent several years studying Earth's comparative religions. We have as many distinct religions as we have earthly sects and there are many, many sects. There is no common religion, but there are several common threads running through most religions.

Most religions believe in an afterlife. Most religions believe in a 'judgment day' that would determine our fates after death. Opinions diverge at that point... Some believe that we return to Earth as another human or as another life form. Some believe that we go to live with God (our equivalent of your Higher Power, I guess). Finally, there is some agreement that persons who have been 'bad' on Earth will never get to see God and / or will receive some level of punishment in the afterlife. It's really very complicated.

But tell me about the Holies. Will I get to meet them?"

Joseph laughed. Surprisingly, his translucent friend seemed to laugh along with him! "None of us get to meet the Holies until we die! Baaners believe that when the Holies first created us, we lived alongside them in a beautiful pasture where the food was plentiful, everyone was healthy, and no one died. Sometime later, we committed some egregious sin, and we were banished from the pasture. We pray to the Holies now hoping that we can return to that glorious pasture when we die."

I was astonished at how closely this paralleled the Judeo-Christian scriptures' writings about the Garden of Eden. What could this mean?

I told Joseph about the Judeo-Christian Bible and the concept of original sin and he too was amazed at our newly discovered coincidence.

Expecting another parallel, I asked Joseph if he wouldn't mind summarizing the Supreme Chieftain's laws, the ones inscribed on the tablet. Joseph named them one by one.

"One cannot worship anything other than the Higher Power
One cannot worship an idol
One cannot use the Higher Power's name in vain
One should worship at least once a week
One should honor his or her father and mother
One cannot murder
One cannot steal
One cannot lie
One cannot be jealous of another
One cannot be jealous of another's property
One should love one another"

We entered into a discussion about the similarities and differences between The Supreme Chieftain's ten laws and our Ten Commandments. We concluded that they were very much the same, except that the concept of 'adultery' was absent in Baaner laws and the "love one another" law was actually similar to the teachings of our Jesus Christ. Joseph pointed out that if you truly respect one another and act out of love, there is no true adultery. I had to think about that one.

I asked Joseph if he and the other Blacknecks believed in evolution. Here was his response:

"Of course, Harry! All scientific evidence supports the theory of evolution. We believe in evolution AND 'intelligent design'. That is to say that the Higher Power created everything, including the process of evolution. Is this not true on Earth?"

"Not quite. Many humans believe that religion and evolution contradict one another. Some take our Bible literally because it is the Word of God and it states that all species were created in seven days. Personally, I believe our Bible has many allegories, the seven-day thing being one of them."

Joseph grinned. I suspect that the same discussions were part of the Baaner culture.

I joined Joseph and his colleagues for evening vespers and a lovely dinner of grasses cooked with herbs from their garden. The next day came. Joseph borrowed the community Trigo and drove me over to a building about a one-hour drive away.

"I come here once a week," said Joseph. "This is where many of the aged Baaners go when their families are no longer able to care for them."

There were three long hallways extending out from the entrance foyer. Each hallway had many doors that opened up into rooms, each containing between two and four elderly Baaners. The rooms' walls had the same decorations: murals of grass-strewn pastures. The occupants in each room were either sitting in soft jabberwool chairs or sleeping in simple jabberwool cots. To my surprise, Joseph knew each and every one by name!

Joseph's visitation routine was simple enough. He would knock on the door, walk in, greet everyone individually, and then introduce me. He would ask each Baaner how they were doing, and then offer up a short prayer.

Our visits went without incident for a while. Most of the time the elderly Baaners would acknowledge my presence, bow slightly, and make a short comment about the day's weather. And then we met Lucy.

Lucy was a diminutive ewe covered with bright white wool. She grabbed her cane and rose from her seat.

"So, you're from Earth, eh? I think I remember you. Didn't you visit several years ago? I remember your spaceship very well! You and your Earthlings abducted me and flew around Baa in your spaceship. You had me lie down on a table and experimented on my body. You touched my private parts. It was terrible, just terrible. You should be ashamed of yourself!"

I was aghast. Joseph made some sort of excuse and then we left the room. "Medications", he said. "It happens all the time."

With that, we had a good laugh. We went on to visit another thirty or so elderly Baaners, then went back to Joseph's abbey.

After the evening's vespers and dinner, I was the guest speaker for Joseph and his Blackneck associates. Joseph introduced me...

"Good evening, my brethren. Harry and I have had long talks in which we compared our religion and our relationships with the Higher Power and Holies to the belief systems on Harry's planet Earth. There are indeed very many similarities. I'll not go into great detail now but write a detailed report after Harry leaves us and continues his travels. Please welcome Harry from Earth."

All of Joseph's brethren rose from their seats and gave me the usual chorus of "baahs." I gave a quick summary of the conversations I had had with Joseph and then opened the session for questions. One of the more interesting questions came from Arthur, one of the more senior Blacknecks.

"Perhaps you could tell us, Harry, about some of the more controversial topics on your planet: Areas where humans, religious authorities, and legal systems have constant disagreements."

I had to pause and walk around the podium. This was not an easy topic, but I gave it my best shot...

"First off, we believe in the separation of church and state. While many of our laws are based on the Ten Commandments, we have no discussion of religions in our schools or public buildings. We do not wish, for instance, to discuss one religion because it might offend those who have another religion or none at all."

Arthur interrupted me. "How do your children develop their faiths then? Is it done in their homes?"

"I'm afraid that is a problem. Most parents work and do not have the time to indoctrinate their children in any faith. They send their children to school for others to teach them about religion, but most then come home and see their parents not reinforcing the religion's messages. Further, they just let children choose their own faith when they become adults."

"And do they?" Asked Arthur.

"Not usually. That is why we have more and more agnostics and atheists. I personally think it's very sad."

There was a groan in the audience. I shifted gears and went to another topic. "Another point of controversy is the use of 'abortions' or the process of willfully terminating a pregnancy in the early stages. Many of those of faith believe that life begins with conception and that abortion is an act of murder. Many females, however, believe that they should have control of their bodies and abort a pregnancy if they so choose."

Arthur chimed in again. "This is madness! Life does begin at conception. The conception of a child is one of our greatest blessings. Why would someone ever want to negate such a blessing?"

"I agree," I said tactfully. "It's worse than that. Many humans employ devices or medications that disallow conception. We call this 'contraception.' Many humans may think themselves unready for a child and do not want to burden themselves with an unwanted offspring."

"Unbelievable! How selfish! Our Higher Power wants us to have as many children as we are capable of having. It would be unnatural to behave otherwise. I suppose it's proper then to take your own life. You own your body, correct?"

The questions were becoming contentious and I was ill at ease for the first time. Thinking back to my divinity education, I responded thusly...

"Religious humans believe that our body belongs to God, not to us. With that thinking, abortions, suicide, and euthanasia (the killing of the elderly) should be sinful. With the separation of church and state, however, all of these acts are condoned."

More groans in the audience. I was most uncomfortable and, for the first time, thinking objectively about our culture, the separation of church and state, and the perhaps inhuman acts that come about as a consequence of that separation. Maybe the Baaners had it right.

The next day, Joseph offered to drive me over to the home of Charlene and her "0 sect" family. I was looking forward to learning about the "normal" Baaners. It might be a refreshing change after all of these strongly different views. Maybe?

Chapter 11: The Search for Normalcy

Joseph and I arrived at Charlene's family home just in time for supper. Charlene invited Joseph to stay and dine with her family, but he declined, saying that he needed to get back for evening vespers.

Charlene introduced me to her family. There was George, her mate, and three lambs: Bella, Charlotte, and Danny. Bella and Charlotte were identical twins, I was told. Charlene's family of five lived in a small, humble dwelling, a farmhouse, situated in the middle of their pasture. They evidently grew a variety of farmable grasses and had a small herd of jabbers that they raised for meat and jabberwool.

As was the case with Leroy and his family, we sat down around a wooden table outside of their home for a traditional jabber meat barbeque. We joined hands as George said grace:

"Higher Power, we thank thee for our blessings and your love for us despite our faults. We thank thee for this time with our alien friend Harry and we pray for Harry and his safe travels. Amen."

I was honored to be in their prayers. But, as George led his family in prayer, I could not help but notice one of those translucent apparitions walking around the table and smiling. I knew better than to say anything, so I just thanked George and dove into the food. They did not drink Haykick but, instead, served grasswater from the grasses in their pasture.

George and Charlene led a simple and happy life, living off of the land and raising their three children. Their lives must have been like those of Earth's early settlers: hardworking, family-oriented, and deeply religious. Where had we gone wrong? How did we lose those simple values? Was Charlene right when she appeared on the Baabaa News Hour and asked if the media was responsible for leading Earthlings astray? Was our movement away from God responsible? Food for thought as we were eating, but I digress.

It turned out that George had a really good sense of humor. As we dined, he told many Baaner-specific jokes. Most of the jokes meant nothing to me, but they sure made the children laugh heartily. I had to laugh, not at the jokes but at the 'kids' rolling on the ground and retelling each of George's jokes to each other. I thought you might like a sample of George's Baaner humor:

"What do you call a Baaner covered in chocolate? Candy baa.

What do you call a dancing Baaner? A baa-lerina!

What do you call a Baaner with no limbs? A cloud.

Where do Baaners get their wool cut? At the baa-baa shop!

Where do Baaners take a bath? In a baaaa-th tub!"

Funny, huh? Even Baaners think they could look like clouds without their limbs. Sitting down with Charlene, George and family was a refreshing change after the heavy-duty intellectual discussions I had previously with Joseph, Betsy and Clarence.

After Bella and Charlotte retired for the evening, Charlene wanted to discuss a family problem: bullying in Charlotte's classroom. Charlotte had recently come back from school in tears, complaining that some of her lamb friends were joking about her and insinuating that she was overweight and ugly. Charlene asked me if bullying was a problem back on earth. My response was that it had been, from time to time, and that it was dealt with severely in the school systems. The earthlings had no tolerance for bullying.

George was highly protective of his lambs. When we discussed Charlotte's being the victim of bullying, he wanted the most severe punishment for the offending lambs: a one-way ticket to Nowhereland. This, of course, would never happen.

We talked some more, laughed some more and made plans for the next day: Going to watch the twins playing "Hoops" in some sort of competitive match.

****

Bella and Charlotte were all excited the morning of the big Hoops game. As I understood it, they were both members of an Ohmy-sponsored team called "The Ewettes." I tried to understand the rules as Bella explained them to me:

"There's this big field. One team throws while another team blocks. After one team has thrown, they take the field and the other team throws. Whichever team has the fewest throws wins the game."

I had no idea what Bella was talking about, so I humored her. I'd have to watch the game to figure it out.

We rode to the Hoops game in a larger version of a Trigo — it had three wheels like other Trigos but had two seats in front and two rows of three seats in the back. I sat next to George in front; Charlene and the twins sat in the three middle seats, while Danny sat in the center position of the rear three seats. All the way to the Hoops field we sang "Take me out to the Hoops game", a popular song.

Let me describe a Hoops field to you. It is a large field with tall grass and about one hundred yards long and fifty yards wide. There are four large hoops placed in a diamond-shaped fashion in the middle of the field. The hoops seemed to be equally spaced and about thirty yards from each other. On either side of the field were tiered benches — one set for "The Ewettes" and their fans, another set for the opposition ("The Pastureton Princesses") and their fans. After playing the national anthem, the Princesses took the field.

Although each team had eleven players, only four could play at a time. One of the four Princess players was positioned within each of the large hoops.

As Bella, the first of the Ewettes, picked up the ball (a hairy thing about three inches across and covered with jabber hair), the fans on the Ewette side all stomped their feet. The game was starting!

Bella stood just to the right of the "home hoop" and threw the ball just in front of the hoop to her right ("first hoop"). One of the other team's players ran out from her position within the first hoop, picked up the ball, and threw it back to Bella. One of the two official scorers put a big number one on the scoreboard for the Ewetttes, as we chanted, "Come on, Bella." I surmised that the scorer would add one point per throw, whether or not the throw would go through the hoop.

Bella was disappointed in her first throw, but she picked up the ball and threw it halfway to the first hoop. She then ran quickly to the ball and fired it through the outstretched arms of the opposing first hoopster. We cheered "Bella, Bella" as she picked up the ball and threw it halfway to the second hoop. This time, the second hoopster ran to the ball, as did Bella. Bella got there just before the other player, picked up the ball and threw it through a now-empty second hoop. I was just now beginning to understand the strategy. Hoops was an interesting game, somewhere between soccer, baseball, lacrosse, and croquet.

Bella continued her running and throwing, amassing a total of fifteen throws. To finish your "half inning", you'd have to get the hairy ball through all four hoops.

In the bottom half of the first inning, The Ewettes took the field. Bella was stationed in the first hoop, Charlotte in the second hoop, and two teammates in the third and fourth hoop respectively. In watching both Bella and Charlotte, I came to the conclusion that Bella was the faster of the two, but Charlotte was a better "blocker". The first Princess thrower concluded her half-inning with a total of sixteen throws, one worse than Bella.

We got to the top of the ninth and last inning. The score was tied, 171-171, and Bella was the thrower. Trying for what they called an "ace", she winged the ball as fast as she could, aiming for the upper left corner of the first hoop on the fly. The first hoopster leaped high for the ball and touched it as the ball trickled through the hoop, or so we thought.

The first hoopster thought quickly and fired the ball back to Bella even though, from our vantage point, Bella had scored by throwing the ball through the hoop.

Bella jumped up and down and then went crying to the scorer. "What?" She yelled. "It went through the first hoop! She can't throw the ball back!"

The two scorers quickly conferred, then turned to Bella. "I'm sorry, dearie, but we both think the ball was blocked. You'll have to throw again." The scorer then added one point.

A flustered father, George grabbed his glass of grasswater and hurled the contents into the face of one of the scorers. "You are both blind jabbers. That ball went through the hoop!"

Bella ran over to the first hoopster, grabbed her by her wooly hair, and threw her to the ground. "Cheat, cheat! You're nothing but a cheat!"

The benches emptied and the twenty-two ewes were fighting and pulling each other's hair.

The two scorers conferred, and then one of them threw down a red jabbercloth. "Forfeit!" He yelled. "The Princesses win."

George regained his composure and walked over to the chief scorer. "I'm very sorry," he said. "What I did was wrong. The game was played well on both sides. The Ewettes should not be punished. Can't we end the match on a tie?"

And so, the game ended on a tie. Charlotte, in a surprising burst of wisdom, told her father "You can be right in the absolute sense but wrong in your actions. You always tell us that, but you forgot your own advice." I could not help but smile. Smart child...

George apologized to the twins, said it would not happen again, and then promised to take the whole family to the Baaner Fair tomorrow. What was I in for tomorrow?

****

The next day, we piled into the family Trigo again, this time heading for Pastureton's Baaner Fair. It was a grand, warm day for the fair. Their sun shone brightly as we meandered down the main thoroughfare and into downtown Pastureton. Young Danny was particularly excited, jumping up and down in the Trigo's rear seat. He kept singing...

" I went to the Pastureton Fair,
The jabbers were plentiful there.
We drank our grassade while the Jabber Parade
Created a stench in the air."

Finally, we neared the parade grounds. Like the old country fairs back on Earth, the scene was one of organized chaos. I could see carnival rides and mobs of Baaners strolling and laughing. We parked the Trigo in one of the many parking fields and walked over to the fair's entrance. George paid for all of us, of course.

To my dismay, Danny was right about the "stench in the air". The smell of burning methane mixed with the odor from the fields of grazing jabbers. I tried not to breathe through my nose, as the smell was almost more than I could handle.

I went on a few rides with Danny and a few rides with the twins. Some rides were motorized, using methane as the fuel for the motors. My favorite ride, the one that Danny kept wanting to go on, was a ride in which a jabber-drawn cart went around a track three times. I felt sorry for the poor jabbers; as they were pulling our cart, they kept looking back at me, perhaps wondering if I was some long-lost relative. Sad was the plight of the jabbers. If Baa's evolution had worked differently, maybe the Baaners would have been pulling the cart. Shame on me for even thinking that!

We sat on a bench for our lunch break eating a salad of chopped grasses that Charlene had prepared. I was never big on salads back on Earth and did not wish to hurt Charlene's feelings, so I finished my portion and thanked her profusely.

The next big event was the "Old Trigo Show". We took our places in the fair's grandstand while hundreds of beautiful old Trigos drove by, each with a crusty old Baaner proudly waving as he or she drove the vehicle. I marveled at some of the designs of the early Trigos:

Convertibles, trucks, sedans, vans, and station wagons. The most popular color was black, although all the colors of the spectrum were represented at one time or another. Quite a show!

When the last Trigo left the scene, the great parade started. The Pastureton Police Department rode by in their Trigos, followed by bright red "Fire-Trigos" from Pastureton and all of the neighboring towns. Then came rows and rows of elderly Baaners, each row headed by a proud Baaner waving an elaborate jabbercloth flag. Charlene whispered that these Baaners represented their veteran soldiers.

I thought that the parade had ended because nothing was happening for what seemed like an eternity. Then Danny stood and shouted, "Here come the jabbers! Here come the jabbers!"

Sure enough, I could see down the road where dozens of small herds of jabbers were being prodded along by their respective Baaner ranchers. The jabbers were not at all happy at being paraded around. They kept trying to run off but were brought back into alignment either by their ranchers or by small dog-like creatures that nuzzled them back into formation. Every once in a while, one of the jabbers would stop and stare at me, making me most uncomfortable. I wondered if George and Charlene paid any attention to my obvious discomfort.

As the jabber portion of the parade was ending, Charlotte said: "Let's go see the Jabber Race now!"

We walked over to a fence surrounding one of the larger fields and waited for the fair's next event — the Jabber Race. George pulled out a score sheet of some kind and asked me if I'd like to wager some chips. "Come on, Harry. I'll give you odds. How about Old Red? I'll give you 3:1 odds."

"Why not?" was my response. "The score sheet shows 2:1 odds and you're giving me 3:1. Here are ten chips."

There was a group of eight jabbers all lined up at one end of the field. At the other end of the field was the finish line and, at the finish line, a mob of happy Baaners was waving some form of banana-like fruit. The starter Baaner hit the side of a large gong and all eight of the jabbers were off and running.

It was a close race and the crowd was cheering frantically. Although Old Red was the favorite, he lagged slightly behind "His Hairiness", a much younger jabber. The other six jabbers were a good three or four yards behind Old Red and His Hairiness.

As they neared the finish line, it appeared that His Hairiness would win but, with a burst of speed, Old Red jumped on the back of His Hairiness and vaulted over the finish line!

"Well done, Harry! Here are your thirty chips," said George. We all had a good laugh at the manner in which Old Red came through at the end.

Bella took me by the hand and walked me over to a large tent. "This is the Pastureton Arts and Crafts Show, Harry. Will you please buy me something?"

The two of us parted company with the rest of the family and strolled into the show. There were all kinds of handicrafts — everything from exquisite paintings to jabbercloth quilts and wooden toys. Bella and I walked up and down the aisles until she spotted a jabbercloth blanket, stained pink with a picture of downtown Pastureton engraved in its center. I purchased the blanket with my winnings then bought, for myself, a jabbercloth painting of The Supreme Chieftain. The artist removed the painting from the frame so I could tuck it into my briefcase and keep it with me.

Although we were all exhausted, we had to stay for the concert and fireworks. We picked up a concert program, then went to our seats near the main stage and waited patiently.

The orchestra arrived and took their appropriate positions on the stage. The concertmaster and the conductor, Leonardbernwool, followed them. After a loud ovation, the concert began. Charlene whispered to me "You'll like this one."

I did like the first piece. It was a short work that featured percussion instruments and was called "Fanfare for the Common Ram". The orchestra played a few patriotic marches then ended with "The Pastureton Overture", a rousing piece featuring percussion, cannons and ten minutes of impressive fireworks.

It took us a long time to get out of the parking lot and it was very late when we arrived home. I had trouble falling asleep, thinking about the excitement of the day and the "inhumane" treatment of the jabbers. I thought about how "normal" Baaners really knew how to enjoy life. There were lessons to be learned, for sure!

****

It was time to leave my wonderful "0 sect" friends and start my next adventure — traveling to Mesa View, the land of the Technobirds. I gave a hug to Charlene, George, and the children. I waited outside for Jeeves, Clarence's chauffeur, to pick me up and take me to downtown Pastureton. Jeeves, as usual, was his punctual self and greeted me most warmly. As we drove, Jeeves told me a few things about the Technobirds. Here is our recorded conversation:

"Technobirds are very strange creatures, Harry. They are diminutive Baaners with small wings. They do not fly at all and they wear some kind of visual aids. Their basic language is Baaner-like, but they have all of this amazing jargon. I suspect that Clarence will have arranged for a Baaner translator to accompany you."

"One of my automatic translation languages is for the Technobirds. I have not tried it yet but, if I'm lucky, I should not need Clarence's translator.

Also, we have such visual aids on Earth. We call them 'glasses.' What kind of work do the Technobirds do? Who gives them guidance for products?"

"They are very intelligent and very creative creatures. They invent things, as many as one invention per week. Sometimes they watch Holovision to get their ideas, sometimes they do work directly for the Ohmys, but usually, they just do what they want."

"Will I get to see any of their inventions, Jeeves?"

"Yes indeed. You will have to sign an NDA or 'non-disclosure agreement' though. Clarence will show you the terms. It usually specifies that you will not disclose anything that you have seen and that you will not compete for a period of three years. If you violate the agreement, you are banished to Nowhereland."

I had to laugh at the prospects of my ever competing with the Technobirds or, worse yet, doing so within three years and getting exiled to Nowhereland!

We arrived at Clarence's Pastureton residence later that day. Clarence ushered me into his dining area where we enjoyed a dinner of a leg of jabber along with several glasses of Haykick. I told him about my visits, and he listened intently as I did my recapitulation.

I told Clarence about Betsy and as I did so Clarence kept referring to her as a "left-wing liberal" and "out of touch with reality". Being tactful, I did not mention that I shared most of Betsy's views — I just gave an objective narrative of my visit, including Betsy's activities to fight for the rights for ewes to enter the political arena. Clarence's reaction to this was priceless:

"You're kidding, Harry. Our Supreme Chieftain was a ram, the government he formed was comprised of rams, and the whole 'Bigbeard thing' came about because of the emphasis on males. How can ewes grow beards? Ewes are supposed to be tending to the home and raising lambs. Rams are the intelligent ones and the power brokers. It has always been that way!"

I did not mention that Betsy had the largest rear end (and therefore the biggest brain) of all of them. I nodded my head politely and went onto the visit with Joseph.

"Joseph," I said, "is really a holy man. He is very well connected to the Higher Power and to the Holies. One topic that we covered at length was 'separation of church and state.' I told Joseph that, back on Earth, we were paranoid about the separation of church and state and constantly tried to be sure that we had a solid wall between the two. I also told Joseph that I perceived that many of Earth's social problems were due to the rise of atheism and agnosticism and to a parallel loss of faith."

Clarence paced around the room, composing a thoughtful response. "I respect your views on the possible causes of social problems on Earth. I also suspect that Joseph shared your views. But Baa is Baa and Earth is Earth. The Supreme Chieftain provided the House of Baaner Representatives with ten laws that were based on guidance from the Higher Power. It then became the job of the House to create detailed micro-laws that were interpretations of the basic ten laws. In doing so, we needed to be truly democratic and provide for viewpoints other than those worshipping the Higher Power. We have tried to create that separation as much as possible."

It was late and I did not wish to belabor the point with Clarence. I thought to myself that Baaners had created their 'micro-laws' based on the House's interpretation of the basic ten laws and that interpretation was subjective and prone to Baaner error. So be it.

We said our "good nights" and readied ourselves for the long journey to Mesa View. What manner of jargon awaited us? What wild inventions would I see?

Section II: The Land of the Technobirds

Chapter 12: Wild Bill and the Technobirds

Baaners do not have any form of air travel. They drive around in their Trigos or take ships to cross their two expansive oceans, or so I learned from Clarence.

Jeeves drove both Clarence and me to the dock where Lingo.76.33.044675 our translator greeted us. Lingo was a member of Clarence's staff and was specifically trained to act as a translator both for the Technobirds and the Ohmys. He looked a bit like Jeeves and had a sort of faraway look. He spoke very precisely and, in a monotone, much like a robot might speak. For example: "It.is.a.pleasure.to.meet.you. You.are.the.first.alien.I.have.ever.met. I.am.happy.to.help.you.with.the.the.required. translations."

Weird, huh? The three of us stood waiting at the dock, watching the horizon for the arrival of our ship. After maybe a Baaner hour, we could see our vessel approaching from offshore. It looked like one of our old hydrofoils and, as it approached, I detected a strong odor of methane. It was then that I realized that methane was the fuel of choice for all of Baa's vehicles: the Trigos, the ships, and whatever else. I'll let you guess where the Baaners' methane comes from...

The ship's captain lowered the plank and we boarded "Ewess of the Seas" along with several hundred other Baaner tourists. I had to catch myself thinking about the absurdity of all of this. Here I was, on the planet Baa, with several hundred naked sheep-like creatures, taking a ferry to Mesa View to meet with the Technobirds. It was surreal at best!

We stashed our luggage in our separate cabins and then congregated on the main deck to receive training on the use of "life preservers". (Baaners do not swim well, if at all). The captain Baaner announced that our voyage would take three days, during which there was plenty to do: planned activities, and fine dining.

I told Clarence that he and Lingo should enjoy the cruise. I would join them for an occasional buffet meal but would otherwise stay in my cabin and work on my memoirs. I think Clarence was happy to take advantage of a little R&R and I did not want to spend too much time sitting at tables with boring passengers, watching them gawk at me and asking me the same mundane questions: "What is it like on Earth? What did you do for a living? Do you have children? Would you like to see the pictures from our last cruise?" Ugh.

****

We arrived at Mesa View on time, mid-morning three days later. The crew lowered the plank and we joined most of the passengers, grabbing our luggage and descending. Milling about at the bottom of the gangplank were hundreds of these Technobird creatures selling their "trinkets", presumably small inventions that they had crafted.

Let me describe a Technobird for you: I am about six feet tall. Most adult Baaners are about five feet tall and these Technobirds seemed to be about four feet tall. If you remember what Earth's long-extinct "dodo birds" looked like, imagine a dodo bird about four feet tall, covered with wooly fur, with a head more like a sheep, with two small wings, and a large rear-end (like the Knowbies).

It was difficult to ignore the crowds of Technobirds and their creative offerings, but we had to focus on our objectives: Meeting some of the key Technobirds, examining some of their inventions, and setting up trade relationships with Planet Earth. Towards that end, as we waded through the crowds, we noticed one of them holding a sign "Harry, Earthling". We rushed over to where the Technobird was holding the sign and climbed into the awaiting Trigo.

Our first stop was a collection of tall shiny buildings near a large lake. I thought that the exterior of the buildings was glass, but Lingo said that they were probably made of something like Earth's plastic, a material made from methane byproducts. Lingo said that these buildings comprised a "campus" where Bill.77.00.000018 and his staff did their research. Bill, evidently, was a direct descendant of one of the original Technobirds.

One of Bill's assistance, Gladys, met us at the front entrance of the main building and then escorted us up an escalator of sorts to the top floor, all of which comprised Bill's luxurious office. Bill arose from his black jabbercloth chair and had us sit down across from his massive desk. He offered each of us a cool glass of Haykick and then addressed our little party...

"Welcome to Mesa View and to my little campus. I have a brief
time to spend with you before my next meeting. Gladys will take you on a tour of our campus when I leave, but you'll need to sign our NDA."

Bill adjusted his spectacles and extended his hand. "It's good to meet you, Harry. You are the first alien I've had the pleasure of meeting. What questions do you have for me and my staff?"

"Thank you for your time, Bill. I'll gladly sign your NDA. As Gladys takes us around, I'd like to see what technology you have in development and, if there is a potential marketplace back on Earth, set up trade agreements as appropriate. Let me ask two important questions, however. How did you start your enterprise? How did the Technobirds come about?"

"That's the stupidest thing I've ever heard! Everyone knows how the Technobirds started. My great great great grandfather was a famous Knowbie scientist working on genetic research and cloning. He removed three eggs from his Knowbie ewe Martha, altered some of the genetic makeup, fertilized the eggs, and replanted them back in Martha. The rest is history: The first three offspring were the first Technobirds: part Knowbie, part emewe and with the enhanced cerebral matter. Those offspring mated among themselves and our population started to grow."

"And what's an emewe?" I asked.

"A large flying bird. We had hoped that we'd be able to fly, but that never worked out. We just have these short, stubby wings." Bill flapped his wings and adjusted his spectacles again. He continued...

"It was obvious to the early Technobirds that we were a superior species with a new '77' gene pool. They wanted to avoid interbreeding with the normal '76 gene pool' Baaners, so we built great ships and sailed to an uninhabited land that was later named Mesa View. Here we settled and were free to allow our creative juices to flow.

Our first major product offering was a computer program called 'Orifice.' It allowed Baaners to communicate with one another by speaking into their computers. We sold many copies of the program and I became very wealthy, so much so that my ewe Melinda and I started a foundation to improve the Baaners' educational system. I am now the wealthiest on all of Baa."

I couldn't resist asking the next question. "Tell me, Bill. Do your laws permit genetic research and cloning? What would the Supreme Chieftain...."?

Bill became flushed with anger and interrupted: "Another stupid question! There are no laws specifically banning genetic research. I believe that the Higher Power and the Holies want us to be as creative as possible, with no boundaries. How else can you improve the species and become one with the Holies? Surely not by the power of prayer!"

I saw that this was going nowhere. Clarence and Lingo were stirring uncomfortably in their seats. I needed to back off and cater to Bill's enormous ego. "Tell me, Bill. Are there other campuses on Mesa View? Do you have competition?"

Bill looked at me condescendingly. "Of course. There are many other research facilities on Mesa View, and each facility tries to compete with me. I'm bigger and I'm better. Every time a competitive product arises, I build something similar to it in Orifice. It works all the time and we squash all our competitors." Bill smiled triumphantly.

Gladys whispered in Bill's ear and Bill excused himself. "I have to run now. Enjoy your tour of our campus; you're in good hands with Gladys."

Bill left the room as Gladys went to a nearby shelf and picked up a stack of papers — there had to be at least one hundred pages. "Here's our standard NDA, Harry. Please initial each page and sign pages 5, 45, 87, and 91. I'll be back in thirty minutes to take you on the tour."

The document was much more onerous than I expected. Clarence, Lingo and I sat around a table in Bill's office and skimmed each page. Lingo, it seemed, had seen this document before and was able to point out the important parts. There was the usual business about not competing, but Bill had changed the wording from "anywhere on Baa" to "anywhere in the universe". He was well prepared for a visiting alien! I signed and / or initialed all of the pages as Bill had suggested, knowing all too well that he'd never be able to enforce any penalties outside of Baa.

After we gave Gladys the signed NDA, she escorted us to an adjacent building and introduced us to Zelda.77.00.001589. Zelda was the lead, we were told, on their "Wearable Orifice" product.

We sat down in an office with an internal Holovision system. Zelda started the presentation:

"Here is Orifice running on a wearable top and on a wearable bottom."

As she said that, two Technobirds appeared holographically. The first, a female, was wearing a bright red tee shirt. The second, a male, was wearing khaki-colored shorts. Zelda continued... "The two Technobirds appear close to each other in Holovision, but they are actually many thousands of hoofs apart. Watch as they converse with each other..."

Sure enough, the two Technobirds were able to converse with each other effectively. It was a very impressive hands-free communication. Of course, we had something comparable on Earth, but I wished to remain polite to our hostess and did not mention that fact. I did, however, pose one important question after the holograms vanished and Zelda awaited our comments.

"Very impressive, Zelda. I can see why your Orifice product is so successful. Tell me, though, why do you think that 'Wearable Orifice' will be a success if your Baaner customers do not wear clothing? Do you plan any test marketing?"

Zelda, of course, was ready with her answer. "Time-to-market is of the essence. We always rush to get our products out before competition develops. Everyone loves Orifice, so they'll all jump on this product. I have options on thousands of shares of stock and hope to retire after this hits the market."

And so, I complimented Zelda and her team and wished them luck on the product launch. I nodded to Gladys and she was ready to take us to the next prototype.

Could I have been wrong? Would Baaners change their habits and wear clothing simply because the clothing ran the Orifice program and allowed them to converse remotely with one another? Would it not have been a good idea to do some test marketing in the various Baaner sects? I was thinking back to my experiences on Earth, where many new products failed because of a rush to market and without adequate testing. Who was I, a lowly Earthling, to question the wisdom of Bill and his employees? Surely, they knew what they were doing. Or did they?

****

Gladys drove us over to our next stop within the research compound. It was a relatively small structure, very much isolated from the rest of the buildings. As we approached, I could not help but notice the most unpleasant odor emanating from the entrance to the building. Gladys paused to comment before opening the door:

"In this building, we have a team doing extensive research on the repurposing of excrement. As you all know, the Baaners defecate outside in the fields as part of a time-honored social tradition. We technobirds respect their tradition but feel it is more civilized to use a receptacle for our urine and fecal matter."

Gladys opened the door. "At this point, I'd like to introduce you to Shinola.77.00.005645; she is in charge of the research within this facility. Shinola?"

"Thank you, Gladys. We have a number of important research projects going on here. In that corner, for instance, is a sure moneymaker. We call it 'pay2poop'. Let me show you how it works…"

Shinola proudly strutted over to a locked metal shack. She inserted two chips into a slot on the front door and pulled on the door's handle to gain access. Inside was a shiny metal receptacle topped with, I would assume, a jabbercloth seat.

"There," exclaimed Shinola. "What do you think of it?"

I was immediately reminded of our ancient experiences with pay toilets back on Earth and could not resist asking some key questions.

"Impressive, Shinola. What happens if someone has the urge to go and has no chips on himself or herself?"

"We thought of that, Harry. The user just needs to enter their full name on the pullout keyboard to receive a bill mailed to their home. No problem."

"I can see a limited market for this among the technobirds, but how about the Baaners? Would they change their habits and use a pay receptacle or any receptacle for that matter?"

Shinola sported a big grin. "The value proposition for the pay2poop product among the Baaners is this: We, all the inhabitants of Baa, are facing a significant environmental challenge. With the increased burning of methane-based fuels comes an increase in the amount of carbon dioxide in the atmosphere; there have been many studies to show this. Then, as the carbon dioxide levels increase, our atmosphere begins to heat-up, our polar ice masses melt, and our oceans rise. It is happening right now and poses a clear and present danger.

So, Harry, pay2poop collects the waste in large tanks underneath the metal shack. Periodically, the large tanks are emptied, and their contents brought here for repurposing. You'll see this in some of the breakthrough work being done here by my colleagues.

Additionally, all the money collected from the products will flow back to the technobirds to facilitate further research, typically in the area of solar energy sources.

In summary, this revolutionary product will save the planet Baa. Can you now see the importance of this effort?"

Clarence was obviously concerned. "We've been hearing about this climate change stuff for years now. I've seen some of the so-called research studies and I'm not convinced that there is any kind of a problem. No problem, then no marketplace. I cannot see this happening in my lifetime!"

I dared not mention that we Earthlings had seen this problem as far back as the 20th century. We addressed the problem with a set of smart alternative-energy solutions – just in time, I might add.

Shinola chose not to argue with Clarence. She simply waved us on: "In this area, we can see how the pay2poop system provides valuable byproducts. Firstly, see how this filtration system extracts drinkable water from the contents of pay2poop tanks."

She went over to an elaborate machine, a maze of pipes and multi-colored tubes around a whirring motor. Shinola then put a cup under a tap extruding from the filtration device and poured a cup-full of liquid, sipping it enthusiastically.

"Pure, tasteless drinking water from pay2poop waste. Harry, would you care to try it?"

I thought quickly. "No thanks, Shinola. I'm really not thirsty. Maybe later."

Shinola laughed. "Very well then. Now watch this…"

She put a hose over the water tap and plugged the other end of the hose into yet another device. She then pushed a button that invoked more whirring. Small cubes began to tumble out.

"Behold! Dehydrated drinking water in cube form. Another useful option is to dehydrate the drinkable water into easily transportable cubes. You just add water to the cubes to get double the volume of drinking water!"

While I was less than convinced about the utility of this particular invention, I nodded briefly to show my approval. Shinola then went on to show us the third related invention.

"Finally, watch what happens here." Shinola went over to the filtration system and pulled a large lever. Out of the rear of the device popped about a dozen large cubes of solid material. They fell onto the floor. "We even have a system for mining the pay2poop's solid waste. I have just demonstrated how the tanks' solid waste is dehydrated and processed into cubes that can be shipped anywhere to be used as compost. What do you think, Harry?"

I could not say what I really thought. I did think that one of the dehydrated fecal cubes would make a very good keepsake, so I stealthily popped one into my briefcase.

By this time, the smell was really getting to me. How could I convince Gladys that it was time to make our excuses and exit left to pursue other forms of creative genius? I tried: "Bravo, Shinola! You and your team have done a truly amazing job. Your pay2poop product will save the planet, provide funding for your research, provide drinkable water in tap or dehydrated form, and crank out material suitable for compost. Bravo indeed!

This was a most worthwhile stop, Gladys. I cannot wait to see what other major research projects you have in the works in Mesa View. Please lead the way!"

It worked. Gladys motioned us towards the door, and we were on our way.

****

We ambled down a path that eventually led to a glass-roofed structure surrounded by grasses of every imaginable color and size. It was really a sight to behold. Gladys did the introduction:

"As you must know, grasses form the most popular food staple on all of Baa. In this next building, you will see how some of the grasses grown here can be used to produce some very useful byproducts. Let's go in and take a look." Gladys opened the door and ushered us in. She continued...

"This first station is where we create grass-flavored shampoo. While Baaners may never drink this product, they should all be pleased with the scent that this shampoo imparts as they wash their wool. Take a sniff, Harry."

Grass-flavored shampoo? She had to be kidding! But, always the diplomat, I replied that the scent was quite appealing.

Moving right along, Gladys showed us another station at which grass was being machine-processed into "grassy bars", perhaps the equivalent of the protein bars once popular on Earth.

Gladys proudly took one of the bars off of the assembly line and challenged me to try it. "This is one of my favorite products. We call the brand 'Grassy Valley' and there are three, make that four flavors. Won't you try this one, Harry? I think you'll enjoy it as much as I do."

The wrapper was colorful and contained the words "Grassy Valley Grass Bar - White Clover". I carefully removed the wrapper and took a small bite. It tasted as you might expect white clover to taste. There was no sugar content and it was kind of bland. "This is really tasty, Gladys. I'll take the rest home with me to enjoy later if you don't mind."

Gladys smiled, knowing I'd give it the old "heave-ho" at my first opportunity. "Step over here, Harry. This next innovation is going to be a sure-fire success. 'Self-cutting Grass!' What do you think?"

I was looking down on a large table, the top of which was a rectangular container with several inches of soil and, growing out of the soil, a luxurious bed of green grass. "How does this grass work? How does it cut itself?" I asked.

"The grass reaches a height of about one quarter hoof, then automatically stops growing. You never need to trim the grass."

"But," I asked, "If it ceases to grow, will it not wilt in the sun? Will it not lose its color and texture?"

Gladys pondered a moment. "That's quite possible, Harry. We need to run more trials and examine more data. Let me take you now to the last station."

Adjacent to the self-cutting grass table was a large, elaborate machine. At one end of the machine was a large hopper. The hopper fed an array of tubes, pipes, and motors leading, finally, to a belt-fed assembly line.

"Just watch me now!" said Gladys as she grabbed a large bundle of grass and placed it into the input hopper. "When I press this red button, the processing will start, and this grass will become adhesive synthetic wool."

After hitting the big red button, I watched the device swallow the grass and pass the processed material along various tubes and pipes. The motors whirred gently then, at the other end of the machine, there spewed a long stream of light-brown fabric. I had no idea what was going on, so I awaited Gladys' explanation. Gladys pressed the red button again to stop the machine. She then grabbed a pair of shears and snipped a small piece of the fabric being output.

"Touch this, Harry. The top portion of this is synthetic wool; the bottom portion is a proprietary adhesive."

I stared at the fabric, and then passed it on to Clarence and Lingo. "Of what use is this material? What is the marketplace?"

Gladys was ready for this one. "There is a large bubble population of aging Baaners; we call them 'Baby Baaners'. These Baaners expect to lose some, perhaps all, of their wool. With this product, they will be able to snip patches of synthetic wool and give the illusion of youthfulness."

I had to challenge her on this. "But not all Baaners are light-brown. Will you have other colors? White? Black?"

Gladys frowned. "It would be cost-prohibitive to produce the myriad of colors required to match each and every aging Baaner. We can only produce one color - light brown. The Baaners will get used to it and love it. Maybe we'll throw in a bottle of brown dye with each sale so that they can dye their whole bodies to match the patches! They'd rather have patches of light brown synthetic wool than bare pink skin, don't you think?"

"Well, being an alien and not an aging Baaner, I'd prefer to defer to my colleagues: Clarence and Lingo. What do the two of you think?"

Clarence, being the ultimate politician, told Gladys that, speaking for himself and for Lingo, the product would be a great success. He asked for a sample to bring home.

I wondered, yet again, about the large cost of research and about the cost of building these elaborate prototypes. Was there really a market for any of these things on Baa? Who, if anyone, was doing test marketing before the inventions were ready? Was this just 'Bill's Grand Sandbox' where the Technobirds played all day?

Gladys held open the exit door and allowed us to pass through. When we were outside the hothouse, she turned to us... "Let me set your expectations. We have looked at two of our research areas and have several more to go. After we have toured the entire campus, we have a wrap-up dinner scheduled with Bill and Melinda. After dinner, I shall escort the three of you to your lodging. You'll need a good night's sleep because tomorrow we'll start the process of contract negotiations."

My goodness! How much more of this could I take in in one day?

****

We clambered into Gladys' Trigo once again, this time heading to a massive building a few minutes away. The building resembled an aircraft hangar with enormous front doors. We entered through a small door in the rear entrance, however. Gladys continued her tour:

"You might call this the 'odds and ends' building. There are quite a number of prototypes being built, and we'll only have time to see a half-dozen or so. Please follow me."

We started our "show and tell" in one remote corner near the rear entrance. Gladys walked over to a small table.

"Here we have the latest in 'green' technology: a solar-powered flashlight. Watch this..."

91

Gladys flipped the switch, but nothing happened. She tried once again with no luck and then left us to confer with a nearby technician. She returned after a few minutes, with some news: "I'm sorry, everyone. I should have realized that this flashlight only works when it is in direct sunlight. Would you care to watch outside?"

I looked over to Clarence and Lingo. They shook their heads in a negative response. I thanked Gladys, saying that we still had much to look at – if she did not mind. Off we went to the next exhibit...

"This is the area in which we develop Jabber-related technology. This, for instance, is a spring-loaded jabbermeat flipper."

Gladys cocked the spring on the flipper and then placed one of the raw jabbermeat patties on the top surface. She then pushed a button on the end of the handle. The jabbermeat patty sailed, Frisbee-like fashion, landing squarely in Clarence's face. Gladys apologized...

"I'm so sorry, Clarence. I must have pointed the flipper in the wrong direction. Let me try again..."

Clarence grunted. Gladys then repeated the process with yet another jabbermeat patty. This time, the spring fell out of its holder and the patty soared directly overhead, landing unceremoniously on the floor next to me. Gladys was flush with embarrassment...

"I guess this is not yet market-ready. I'll make sure that Bill knows about this problem. Please step over here now..."

Next to the jabbermeat flipper was a blue rickshaw-like cart with long wooden handles in the front, a jabbercloth cabin to hold two passengers, and two shiny wheels.

"This is another answer to the climate-change problem," said Gladys proudly. "We will train jabbers to pull these carts and reduce the methane pollution generated by Trigos. We call this the Jabbermobile."

Clarence reacted quickly. "But jabbers are such stupid animals. They'll go wherever they want to go, not where you want to go. And, do you think this will cut down on methane consumption? I think not. The jabbers will defecate all over our highways and generate just as much methane, maybe more."

Of course, I took umbrage with Clarence's comments. I was certain that jabbers were more intelligent than he had given them credit for. After all, was I not a direct descendant of these creatures? I chose not to comment, however. I remained politically correct.

Gladys looked at the cart and then looked over at me. What was she thinking? I'd better not ask. She did respond to Clarence, however...

"I happen to think that jabbers have the intelligence to support this endeavor. We are planning some road trials in the near future and I'm sure, Clarence, that these trials will prove you wrong. Follow me and we'll see the next demonstration."

Thank you, Gladys! Not too far away from the blue jabbermobile was a table full of what seemed to be shoes of some kind. Gladys picked up a pair and tried them on...

"We call these high hoofs. We feel that these will be trend-setting fashions for the Baaner ewes. Now I know that you'll chastise me again for not going through a test-marketing exercise, but I really feel that these are bound to be quite successful."

I had to ask... "And why do you think they will be worn by my Eweish friends? They do not wear foot apparel of any sort now."

"Simply, Harry, that Baaner ewes wish to be considered as equals to their ram counterparts. These high hoofs will elevate their physical stature and give them heights equal to those of their male counterparts. The increased height given to the Baaner ewes will have a strong psychological effect. They will feel supremely confidant and empowered."

"But what if they slip and fall all the time? That cannot be a confidence builder."

"Trust me, Harry. They'll flock to the stores. Time to invest in our stock!

Come along now. We just have one more stop," said Gladys excitedly. Then our grand dinner with Bill and Melinda."

At the far side of the building, we had noticed a gigantic green tarpaulin covering some kind of project-in-progress. We had given it no thought until now when Gladys brought us alongside. She waved to four Technobird attendants who were obviously awaiting her signal. The attendants pulled on a series of long ropes to remove the tarpaulin and reveal a colossal airship, reminiscent of our bygone dirigibles. As was the case with the blimps of old, there was a small cabin under the airship. Gladys hurried us onboard and into the cabin.

"I've saved the best for last," she said excitedly. "We will ride the airship to give you an aerial view of Mesa View and we'll land the ship back at our headquarters."

One of the attendants got into Gladys' Trigo and attached a towline to the bow of the airship. He then towed us very slowly out of the hangar and into the front parking lot. Once there, another of the attendants jumped into our cabin and took a position at the helm. The towline was released, and we were airborne!

I had my mild trepidations, of course, remembering how the Hindenburg had gone up in flames many centuries ago. I had to ask some questions.

"This is some majestic flying machine, Gladys. What gives the airship its buoyancy? Is it methane?"

"Yes. We filled the ship with methane as you were watching the earlier demonstrations. A methane-powered motor steers the ship once in the air."

"And are there no safety concerns what with a methane balloon and a motor burning methane fuel?"

"We haven't had a problem yet, and I do not anticipate one. This is Bill's favorite toy."

And so, we cruised lazily around the entire island of Mesa View. We coasted over all of the research sites and all of the dormitories and eating facilities. Mesa View was a beautiful island; no wonder it spawned such creative genius.

After we had done our circumnavigation of Mesa View, our captain steered the ship towards Bill's headquarters, now looming large on the horizon. The captain told us not to worry about the smell of methane as he released methane from the balloon's superstructure, into our cabin, and out through the cabin's windows.

The smell was most offensive. I wondered why the methane was not vented directly into the atmosphere. The captain immediately answered that question...

"We designed the airship to release methane through the cabin because I can smell the released gas and determine if it's the correct methane to air percentage for the descent. I've gotten pretty good at it by now!"

Again, I wondered... Why did they not use a gauge instead? What if the captain had a cold and could not smell accurately? What if... what if?

We came down towards the parking lot in front of the headquarters building – a little abruptly, I might add. The airship's nose actually careened into Bill's corporate Trigo before we came to a bumpy stop. We were now onto to the dinner party with Bill and Melinda.

Chapter 13: Bill and Melinda

We climbed the stairs to Bill's executive dining room, an exquisitely decorated room adorned with multiple portraits of Bill, Melinda, and his family. I was seated at the head table between Bill and Melinda. Clarence sat to Bill's right, with Lingo sitting next to Clarence. Tall, cool glasses of Haykick were placed at each table setting. Each table had several vases containing multi-colored grasses. It was most elegant; I felt that I was being treated as a head of state.

When we had all been seated, Bill introduced our little party to his guests, primarily his executive staff and their partners. "Thank you all for joining Melinda and myself on this festive occasion. We are honored to have Harry, the ambassador from Planet Earth, here to view our products and emerging technology. Clarence and Lingo, members of the Baaner House of Representatives, have accompanied Harry. Harry has signed our NDA, so feel free to introduce yourself later on during our breaks.

Tomorrow we will sit together and work out a distribution agreement with Harry, with hopes that the denizens of Earth might prove a fruitful marketplace for our technology. But – that's tomorrow. Tonight, let us eat, drink, and be merry.

We have scheduled some surprise entertainment before dinner is served. Please welcome Elvis.77.00.001776!"

A door opened at the far end of the room as in strolled a strange-looking Technobird. Elvis was somewhat taller than most of the male Technobirds. He had wild, stringy black wool and carried a musical instrument of some sort, somewhat like a guitar.

He bowed to Bill and Melinda and then walked up a ramp to a small platform. There, he started to play the instrument and sing...

"EDCDEEE
DDDEGG
EDCDEEE
EDDEDC..."

This went on for about three minutes, during which I surreptitiously tried all four of my translation channels. Nothing worked! I was completely confused... What was Elvis singing? Was this a private joke of some sort?

The first song ended, and Elvis was treated to a raucous standing ovation. I looked at Clarence; he seemed to be as confused as I. Lingo, who had been virtually silent during our visit thus far, scribbled a note and passed it to Clarence and myself. It read: "Elvis speaks in musical scale letters. You need to be able to understand each letter's note as it is being sung. Be patient and sit tight."

Clarence and I were patient. We sat through Elvis' performance and joined the audience in their cheers every time that they would stop and applaud. Strange. Very strange.

The first (appetizer) course served was roast jabbermeat on skewers. Each skewer had four or five jabbermeat chunks paired with some form of edible tuber. There was a sticky brown dipping sauce made of God knows what. I tried it, however, and found it fairly tasty.

As we awaited the main course, Melinda and I started a conversation on the topic of education. It seemed that Bill and Melinda were committed to improving the Baaners' educational system using a mixture of private funding, prototype educational processes, and Mesa View technology. Much to my surprise, Melinda had actually authored an educational book entitled "How to Read a Book".

I told Melinda that the Earthlings had slowly improved the educational system to the point where most everything was done online. Melinda then commented: "We are committed to that same sort of transformation. The technical underpinning for the educational system we are rolling out in prototype form is, of course, our flagship Orifice product. We are committed to supplying each underprivileged lamb with a small computer running Orifice in combination with a rich set of education-oriented apps."

My cynical self-thought that this was a clever way of making Orifice ubiquitous on the entire planet Baa. Start 'em early and get 'em hooked. Right? I ignored that point and asked a more fundamental question... "Many of the underprivileged Baaner lambs probably have little or no experience with computers. How does your educational system overcome this obstacle?"

Melinda must have anticipated this question, so she took out a small tablet device. "Watch this," she said.

Melinda randomly pressed a few buttons and then, on a bright blue-tinted screen, came the text "0xc0000225".

Melinda then spoke into the computer's microphone. "Please help me with error 0xc0000225." and the computer responded: "You have an irrecoverable error. Please contact your system administrator."

Melinda smiled. "See how easy it is if you run into any kind of procedural error. We have carefully engineered Orifice to provide many levels of quality online help! If you don't mind, I'll give you a short demonstration of the power of Orifice."

Melinda swiftly ran through the Orifice functionality. Like our cellular phones on Earth, Orifice had a touch screen, could easily be used to converse with another party, and had thousands of readily available applications.

I nodded with my (tentative) approval. Just then the main course arrived. It was a leg of jabber with mint sauce, accompanied by steamed grasses.

Given the fact that we had never discussed product pricing, I tactfully brought up the topic. Bill's response surprised me:

"The Orifice product is priced competitively. We have a wholesale price to the Ohymys who, in turn, develop a retail price for their distribution channels to the other Baaners. When Speaker Tramp was in office, he introduced tariffs on our products as they were shipped to the Ohmys. The tariffs just did not work. The Ohmys just increased their retail prices and our business suffered. When Speaker Tramp was banished to Nowhereland, the tariffs were abolished."

During the course of the evening, many of Bill's executive staff came over to introduce themselves. I will not bore you with any of the details – mostly they were just curious, just wanting the opportunity to say that they had conversed with Harry, the alien from Earth.

When the festivities ended, I thanked our hosts and went with Gladys to my guest bedroom. I'd try to get a good night's sleep before tomorrow, a full day of important negotiations.

****

I met with Bill and members of his staff for breakfast. We had a polite conversation about climate change issues and how those issues had been resolved back on Earth.

Bill was anxious to start our negotiations even at this early hour, so I mentioned that I'd need my briefcase, that I had left it in my room. Not wishing to break the flow of conversation, Bill asked Alfred.77.00.000899, one of his staff, to fetch my briefcase.

The breakfast conversation, in the interim, turned to the subject of work ethics. Bill was the third-richest inhabitant of Baa and had achieved that status with his intellect and with his extraordinary drive. He expected no less from each and every employee: Intelligence, dedication, and commitment to put in whatever hours were required to get the job done. He even said, "Life is not fair; get used to it!"

I admired this trait and was somewhat envious of his success. I told Bill that Earthlings were once hard working and industrious but, over time and with the advent of some technology, that trait had withered away. I told him that the young Earthlings expected an easy job and immediate wealth after graduating from college.

Just then, Alfred returned with my briefcase. He seemed extremely concerned about something as he whispered something in Bill's ear. Bill and Alfred excused themselves from the breakfast table and went off, with my briefcase, to confer. Everyone seated at the table was most puzzled – what was going on?

Bill came back after about ten minutes. He was flushed with anger. He paced around the table and finally spoke...

"We have a major problem here. I would like everyone to leave the room except Harry."

Clarence quickly interrupted. "If there is a problem, Bill, we need to hear about it. We are both Harry's escorts and advisors."

"So be it," said Bill, slamming his fist on the breakfast table and knocking over two of the vases. "While in Harry's room, Alfred inadvertently opened this briefcase. Look at this! A competitive product and, to make things worse, some proprietary output from our waste product processing system. What do you have to say about this, Harry?"

In all of my days on Baa, I had never experienced this level of anger. In order to stay in Clarence's good graces, I needed to remain calm in the face of this storm. I responded... "This is a cube of fecal matter which dropped on the floor during Shinola's demonstration. While you may not agree, I DO know shit from Shinola."

I looked back at Bill. I grabbed the cube of fecal matter and placed it on the breakfast table. "This is just one of Shinola's droppings. I just wanted to bring this back to Earth to amuse my friends."

Bill wiped the offensive matter off the table. "Alright. So, this was a harmless keepsake. But how do you explain THIS?"

Bill took my cell phone out of the briefcase. Admittedly, it looked very much like the small hand-held computer that ran his Orifice software. Evidently, Alfred had powered it up and concluded that it was a competitive product. Explaining this might be difficult, but I tried...

"This is my cellular phone; I brought it with me from Earth. I have not seen all of the functions of Orifice demonstrated, but I assume that it has much of the same functionality as my cell phone. Cell phones are used, back on Earth, to communicate between Earthlings both with sound and with video. As is the case with Orifice, these devices also perform a myriad of useful functions. To be honest, I'd be lost without it. Surely, you do not object to my bringing my cell phone with me?"

"But I do object!" Bill maintained his fury. "I'm sure that you've come here to study Orifice and steal our proprietary user interface! Our tour is over. There will be no negotiations. Pack your stuff and get out of Mesa View!"

Clarence, Lingo and I all stared at each other. There was no communicating with this buffoon. While I was too angry to comment, Clarence took charge:

"We will contact the ferry and arrange for a pickup later today. Speaking for Harry, Lingo and myself, I'm truly sorry for any misunderstanding. We came here with the best of intentions. Please believe me."

Bill said nothing more. He stormed out of the room and there was nothing left to do but plan our hasty exit. While on the ship going to Corporus, the land of the Ohmys, Clarence and I would recapitulate the Mesa View fiasco while making our plans for the visits with the Ohmy giants. I was sure that I'd have better luck there!

Section III: Corporus, the Land of the Ohmys

Chapter 14: The Cruise to Corporus

The ferry picked us up later that day. We retired early and without an evening meal, instead planning to discuss our experiences over breakfast.

So, Clarence, Lingo and I sat at the breakfast table wondering how things went so badly so quickly. With my knowledge of psychology on hand, I surmised that Bill had more than a touch of paranoia. Clarence and Lingo agreed with this and we concluded that it was useless to waste any ergs of energy on dysfunctional Mesa View. Better to do a good job on Corporus.

I wanted to discuss Corporus. What were the inhabitants like? How did they conduct business? What was their marketplace? What was their relationship with the Baaners? With Mesa View? I had so many questions! Here is the transcription of the conversation with Clarence:

"You know, Harry, the Ohmys are very different. They speak the same dialect as the Baaners, but they have a wide variety of idiomatic expressions. You probably thought that it would be a waste of Lingo's time to come along on this trip but, I assure you, we are going to need his help quite frequently. I do not know if your automatic translation device will even help you.

The Ohmys were once Baaners; you'll be surprised to know. They're like just like us but are much larger, initially gaining their grand stature by toying with their pituitary glands. Legend has it that, when the first Baaners became successful at business, they wanted to isolate themselves from the masses, so they moved to the Isle of Corporus. They continued interbreeding and building their population by pituitary manipulations. The rest is history, as they say!"

I had more questions. "Tell me then, what products do they produce and what do they consider to be their marketplace?"

"Did I mention that they wear clothing? I guess I forgot that important point! They have facilities all over Corporus and they produce everything from apparel (for themselves), to toys and Trigos. They see their marketplace as themselves, the Baaners, and the Technobirds."

"Do they interact with alien civilizations? Will there be an opportunity for trade agreements with Earth?"

"We'll need to do some digging here. I've heard a rumor that they seek labor sources outside of Baa, looking for the cheapest possible labor supply. As it relates to your second question, I'd be surprised if you did not come back with a few major trade relationships."

"OK. I understand that Baaners and Technobirds are customers for various Ohmy concerns. Are they also sources of labor for the Ohmys?"

"Yes and no, Harry. The Ohmys tend to seek skilled labor from within Corporus, but they will frequently tap the Baaners for unskilled labor. The Technobirds supply technology to the Ohmys who, in turn, wrap that technology into products.

Incidentally, there are numerous Ohmy enterprises for us to visit, affording you many opportunities for negotiations and deal cutting. We'll be on Corporus for quite a while!"

"I did not bring any clothes with me, Clarence! What should I do? Will they expect me to be in my finery?"

Clarence laughed heartily. "Don't worry. They know that Baaners and their guests come naked. If you like, however, you can invest in some clothes at some of the portside stores when we dock."

****

We docked in the Corporus main harbor in the city of Baaston late the next day. Many tall glass skyscrapers surrounded the wharf. Some seemed to be office buildings while others contained shops. If Baaners were four to five feet tall, the Ohmys seemed twice that height. They hustled about the streets walking or driving in their (much larger) Trigos. Clarence had been correct – all of the male Ohmys were wearing fine suits and some form of jabbercloth shirts with bowties. The female Ohmys were even wearing business suits or dresses! Even the Baaner dockhands were adorned in colorful finery. I felt much as Adam and Eve did when they were first aware of their nakedness! I implored Clarence to stop at the first clothing store we encountered. We entered the store called "Schnook Brothers".

As soon as we walked in, a distinguished looking Ohmy greeted us. He was wearing a dark blue pinstriped suit with shiny silver-colored buttons His white wool was finely manicured. He wore a white shirt and a polka dot bowtie. "Good afternoon. My name is Chesterfield.81.00.029987. How may I help you?" were his first words.

Clarence was kind enough to respond... "My colleague Harry is an alien from Planet Earth. He will be visiting many of the Ohmy enterprises in the next few weeks and will need appropriate clothing. What can you do for him?"

Chesterfield looked me up and down several times. He never cracked a smile. "You are too tall for Baaner clothing and too short for Ohmy clothing. Nothing we have on our racks will suit you, so to speak. But we have a staff of highly skilled tailors who will be able to cobble something together while you wait. Please walk with me over to our fabric section. You can choose anything you like. One of our tailors will then fashion appropriate clothing for your tour."

And so, we walked to where the fabrics were stored. Chesterfield introduced me to Abe.81.00.009354 and then went back to his role as maitre'd / greeter. Lingo, it turned out, had a good sense of fashion. He picked out an off-white fabric for my shirts, a range of pastel-colored bowties, and three fabrics for the suit-making process: blue pinstriped, gray pinstriped and solid black. We showed it all to Abe who then took my measurements with painstaking care. Abe advised that we go out for dinner and come back just before closing time. He would have one suit ready tonight and the others two days later. Impressive!

Clarence asked Chesterfield if we might use the changing rooms before going out for dinner. He obliged, of course, permitting Clarence and Lingo to take some eveningwear out of their suitcases and dress up for dinner.

There were two restaurants nearby: Ruth's Jabber House and Stage Café. The Jabber House sounded good, but we opted for the Stage Café, renowned for its sandwiches.

You had to imagine the next scene. The three of us walked into the Stage Café. There were probably two or three hundred meticulously dressed Ohmys sitting at tables and eating their dinner. Both males and females were present – the males in their fine suits and the females in evening gowns. They all stopped eating and stared as I walked in. Here I was, the first Earthling alien to visit the Isle of Corporus and, to boot, as naked as a jaybird.

What would you do if you were sitting in a fine restaurant eating a meal with your significant other when, all of a sudden, a naked alien casually walked in? I had to put myself in their position. I frankly do not know what I would do!

To my surprise, the diners gave me a quick visual check and then went on with their business – talking and laughing.

We were escorted to a remote corner at the far end of the restaurant, near the families with children, and perhaps to be insulated from the main body of diners.

When we were seated, one of the child Ohmys got up from her table. She looked me over a few times and said "Hello. My name is Lizzy. What's your name?"

I smiled upon getting the warm reception. "My name is Harry. I come from a planet far away."

"You look funny. A bit like a jabber."

I knew that other Ohmys might have had the same thought. I regained my composure... "That may be true, Lizzy. Our planet is called Earth and it's very much like yours. Many, many years ago we walked around just like jabbers. We evolved over time and now we think, walk, and talk just like you!"

I gave Lizzy my business card and that seemed to satisfy her. She went back to her table and, I would guess, went on and on about her encounter with Harry, the alien from Earth. It made my day!

Leonard.81.00.004213 introduced himself as our server. He was wearing a suit partially covered with an apron-like garment. He brought three menus over; each one filled with descriptions of tasty morsels and each menu at least four hoofs tall. "This should keep you busy for a while. Give me a nod when you're ready to order." With that, he walked off.

The three of us joked about the menu. So many choices! We said that we'd share appetizers, so we ordered grass-ball soup and stuffed jabber intestines (a local favorite). For our main course, I chose a sandwich aptly named "The Ohmy Delight" – with a name like that, how could I miss?

Clarence and Lingo ordered a much more conservative offering: "Stage Jabber Patty Sandwich". We ordered also our first round of Haykicks.

We talked for a while but spent most of our time "Ohmy watching". Clarence had mentioned that this café was popular with the Ohmy celebrities. In fact, he said excitedly "That's Ladybaabaa over there! She's the undisputed Ohmy 'Queen of Pop'. Come with me, Harry. I'll introduce you."

I was somewhat uncomfortable. Here I was just getting used to the Ohmy culture when Clarence had me being introduced to a major celebrity. All in a day's work!

Ladybaabaa was dressed flamboyantly. She was in a revealing satiny red dress adorned with bling of every size and shape. She would certainly stand out in a crowd! She was with a male companion, intensely in conversation. That did not stop Clarence, however. He interrupted Ladybaabaa in mid-sentence. "Excuse me, Ladybaabaa, My name in Clarence.76.01.000278 and I'm a member of the Baaner House of Representatives. I did not wish to interrupt your conversation, but I thought you might wish to meet a real alien: my friend Harry from Planet Earth."

A startled Ladybaabaa turned to look at me. "Good to meet you, Harry from Earth. Do you sing, dance, or write music?"

Somewhat nervous, I responded. "My pleasure, Ladybaabaa. I am here on business, trying to set up trade agreements with some of the major players on Corporus. Clarence has told me about your music, though. Perhaps I could distribute your music to the Earthlings when I return. We could establish a lucrative royalty arrangement."

Ladybaabaa thought about this briefly and then responded... "That might be possible, Harry, but my thoughts were not related to distribution rights. I was thinking of doing an album with you – something like 'Ladybaabaa and the Alien'. What do you think? I would write the music and, if you could not carry a tune, we could have you lip-sync. What about that idea? We'll work something out. This is my agent, Frederick.81.00.001976 and here is his card, so please contact him."

I was blown away! An album with Ladybaabaa! I told Ladybaabaa that I used to sing in the choir at college and that my voice was not all that bad. I said that I'd give it a try and that I'd contact Frederick to coordinate our schedules. I thanked Ladybaabaa for her time and went back to our table.

Lo and behold, our food was ready. Let me describe my sandwich, "The Ohmy Delight". It was about three hoofs high. A slice of bread, a thick layer of chopped grasses, another layer of sliced jabbermeat, melted soy cheese, more grasses, more jabbermeat, more soy cheese, and a slice of bread on top. How in the world could I finish this monstrosity! Parenthetically, the sandwiches that Clarence and Lingo had ordered were not quite as big, only two hoofs high.

We ate what we could, and then Clarence asked Leonard for three take-home containers. Perhaps our hotel would have refrigeration devices in our rooms.

Clarence paid our bill and we hustled back to Schnook Brothers, getting there just before their closing time. Abe was standing by the door holding a magnificent dark blue pinstriped suit. I thanked him profusely, taking the suit over to one of the many dressing rooms. It fit perfectly, as did the shirt and one of the bowties.

Abe acknowledged that getting shoes would be a fruitless exercise. All of the shoe stores carried footwear that covered hoofs, not human feet. Of course, he was correct. I would have to wear my fine suit while going barefoot. The cost of doing business on an alien planet!

Clarence paid the Schnook Brothers bill (I wonder how many chips it cost; it must have been an expensive transaction). He told me that all of our expenses would be reimbursed, the source of funds being the House of Representatives' Department of Commerce budget.

We carried our suitcases and walked over to Tramp Towers, our hotel two blocks away. I wore my new suit, of course.

The Tramp Towers in Baaston had a fabulous, majestic interior dripped in gold, a beautiful waterfall, and a meticulously maintained atrium. It was luxury at its best. The public concourse consisted of a gift shop, bar, grille, ice cream parlor, and coffee shop. I was told that it was personally built by Tramp, the previous Speaker of the House. It was a very special feeling to be able to enter the building owned by Tramp and use the same escalator as he did!

Even if you get only a coffee there it's surreal to get it from the place that was home to the most powerful man in all of Baa. Tramp Tower was mesmerizing, the spectacular crown jewel of modern architecture. This was a big change after my stay in the spartan accommodations of Baanerland!

An elderly Baaner employee of the hotel greeted us and took our baggage to our rooms. Clarence gave him a four-chip tip and we settled in for the night. Each room did have a small refrigerator, so we were able to successfully store our Stage Café leftovers.

Tomorrow morning, we would meet our escort, Sheepla.81.00.005895. She would take us our tour of the major enterprises on Corporus.

It was hard to imagine that our days on Corporus would be any more exciting than this, my first day on the isle!

Chapter 15: Sheepla and RalphLawn

We had our continental breakfast and waited in the lobby for Sheepla to arrive. The lobby was awash with Ohmys, all in their corporate finery and scurrying about like agitated mice. Finally, a female Ohmy walked in carrying a sign that read "Harry from Earth". I knew it must be her.

Sheepla was a stunning blondewool, dressed impeccably in a dark gray business suit and wearing the Ohmy version of glasses. She was quite young, I thought, for this awesome responsibility. We waved to Sheepla, and then she crossed the lobby to greet us.

"Good morning everyone. My name is Sheepla.81.00.005895 and I'll be your guide for a number of days while we tour the Isle of Corporus. I have my Trigo waiting outside but are there any questions before we depart?"

I did have a couple of questions. "Hello, Sheepla. I was wondering how you came up with the list of target enterprises. How were they selected and where are we starting?"

Sheepla thought about this for a split second and then responded: "I went through the list of Ohmy enterprises by industry, choosing the top three candidates, by revenue, from each industry sector. I then contacted the Vice President of Marketing in each company and asked if they'd be willing to discuss potential trade agreements with an alien. As soon as one vice president accepted my invitation, I went on to the next industry. In some cases, competitive corporations heard about my efforts and gave me an unsolicited call asking that they are included. I granted those unsolicited requests because they took the time to act proactively. As of now, we have about twenty corporations to visit in fifteen industry sectors. That, of course, is subject to change.

Today, Harry, we are going to visit RalphLawn, one of the top apparel manufacturers on Corporus. I'm sure they'll give us a good jabber circus. Let's get going; my Trigo is running at the front entrance."

Lingo handed me a note: "'Jabber circus' means demonstration and discussion." I thanked him. Meanwhile, I thought to myself, this Sheepla really knows her stuff. Thanks to her, I suspect that this visit will be much more successful than my trip to Mesa View.

RalphLawn Enterprises was just a short drive away. Sheepla pulled into the parking lot where we were met by an entourage and escorted into a lavishly decorated meeting room.

"A feast for the eyes" I whispered to Clarence. "There are carefully coordinated bright fabrics covering the chairs, the lamps, and table decorations. Even the artwork on the walls is coordinated!"

We took our seats in front of a large glass conference table. Each table setting consisted of a nametag, a glass of grasswater and an exquisitely designed napkin. A large plate with appetizers was placed, carefully spaced, between every three table-settings. Even the appetizers were color coordinated!

Xavier.81.00.003111, the Vice President of Marketing, introduced himself. We then went around the table with our own introductions. Xavier started his presentation, abetted by flashy video accompaniment.

"A hearty RalphLawn welcome to our honored guest from Earth. Sheepla has told us of your objectives and we welcome a candid discussion. I thought that a suitable format for this meeting would be (1) A corporate overview (2) Our view of potential synergism, (3) Discussion and action items. Please feel free to pose questions at any time. Let's start with the first slide...

RalphLawn is the largest apparel enterprise on all of Baa. Our revenues are close to eight billion chips per year and we are highly profitable.

Our products fall into three categories: (1) Apparel – both male and female (2) Home furnishings (3) Fragrances.

We do not manufacture any of our products; all of the production is outsourced, with some of the production sources being on Baa, but the majority being on nearby planets.

Our revenue sources, in priority order, are The Ohmys (70%), the Baaners (20%), the Technobirds (5%), and alien planets (5%). We are most interested in expanding our markets to other planets, hence our enthusiasm for meeting with you. Questions so far?"

I jumped right in. "This is most interesting. Am I to assume that the apparel market is restricted to the Ohmys? Also, your home furnishings and fragrances are sold into all four marketplaces?"

"Yes. That is mostly true. We sell virtually no apparel to the Baaners, Technobirds, and aliens. Our home furnishings and fragrances generate revenue in all four customer segments but still – the Ohmys do most of the spending. We'd like to change that.

You may have observed that the Baaners are reluctant to wear any manner of clothing; we are unlikely to change that behavior. The Technobirds not only shun clothing, they never seem to bathe. Did you notice their body odors while on Mesa View?"

I laughed out loud. "Now that you mention it, yes! We were so busy that I did not give it a second thought. Would they not be a decent market for your fragrances though?"

Now it was Xavier's turn to laugh. "It would be like putting perfume on a jabber! We tried but never had any luck. I should add that aliens seem to like some of our home furnishings but generally lack interest in our fragrances."

"May I please ask one more question? Why is it that most of your production is done on other planets? Is it the cost of labor?"

Xavier paused for a moment. "This is a complex question and I'll answer it as best I can.

Yes, it's about labor costs. We do hire a few production personnel from among the Ohmys, and this workforce is unionized. Labor on other planets is much less expensive and we need to keep our costs down to be competitive and offer our shareholders a return on investment. Parenthetically, the Baaners are more interested in agriculture than manufacturing and the Technobirds, as you may have noticed, are in their own little world."

"But how do you control quality if the labor sources are on other planets?"

"Good question. The answer is our quality control methodology. We invest heavily in quality control, putting skilled experts at each production node to ensure the quality of the product prior to shipment to Baa. If I may continue?"

I nodded approval and Xavier went on. "Let me get into our competitive advantages... Next slide?

This is the exciting part. One major competitive differentiator is our design process. We run focus groups each season and in each customer segment. The focus groups keep us in touch with the latest fashion trends and allow us to test market new patterns and fragrances before we go into production. We invest heavily in these focus groups and in our quality control. Good design inputs and top-quality outputs. Next slide?

Color modification is our real strength. We have patented technology, built by the Technobirds, that allows us to modify the color of a fabric AFTER is has gone through production. Let me demonstrate."

Xavier opened the conference room door to admit an attractive, slender female Ohmy wearing a stunning tri-colored dress. It was a paisley pattern, with complementary shades of blue, turquoise, and green. She looked over to Xavier...

"Please meet Alice.81.00.000543. She is one of our top models. Now watch this. Name your favorite three colors, Harry..."

I answered "red, orange, and black". Xavier wheeled over a large silver Rube Goldberesq machine. He carefully clipped one end of a long probe to Alice's dress and the other end to the contraption. He turned a dial and hit the "start button". "There!" he said. "All of the blue has changed to black."

Xavier moved the probe to a turquoise section of the dress and repeated the process, this time turning all of the turquoise to red. He did this once again and green became orange. I was astounded and applauded enthusiastically.

Xavier looked straight at me. "What do you think of that, eh? A real shift of the herd!"

(Lingo passed me a note: "Shift of the herd = behavior change")

"Amazing! I've never seen anything like it. Where do you place these machines? In the production facilities? At the points of sale?"

"We are highly protective of this technology and do not want it ever to get into the wrong hands. While we generally trust our alien production partners, we fear that they might reverse-engineer our color modification technology. To play it safe, we keep this technology restricted to our Ohmy warehouses."

I was really curious now... "That would imply that these fabrics are both synthetic and sensitive to electrical impulses, correct? Can you do the same with jabbercloth?"

"Yes, to the question about synthetics, but I'll say no more on this if you don't mind. And no, we cannot do the same with jabbercloth. Jabbercloth comprises only 30% of our fabric mix.

Let me show you two more slides...

Here is a diagram of our sales channels. We sell our products to both wholesalers and retailers. We even sell online and have our own stores and outlets. We have all of our bases covered, as you can see."

I had to ask... "Do you not have channel conflicts then? Your online channel competing with retailers, for instance?"

"We do, Harry. RalphLawn is so big and so important that we get away with it. Everybody wants our products! Next slide, please?

This last slide shows how we drive sales to help our channel partners. We have a diverse set of programs with a heavy emphasis on cooperative marketing, where we split the marketing expense with our downstream channel partners.

We feature a different female and male model every year in our marketing material. You had the pleasure of meeting Alice, our female model for this year. She has a male counterpart, of course.

Here, for instance, are some printed promotional flyers tailored to our channels and featuring our top models, Alice and Bradley."

Xavier passed the flyers around. It was obvious to me that some photograph modifications had taken place. Believe it or not, Alice was sometimes in her slender form and, on other occasions, quite heavyset – perhaps appealing to an overweight population. Was it ethical, I thought, to modify poor Alice to suit the audience? I'd better not ask.

Xavier paused again, this time to discuss RalphLawn's suggested relationship model for Planet Earth. "So, Harry, this is what we were thinking of for your planet. Next slide?

We would strongly suggest that should we partner; you would establish our focus group methodology for test marketing. We would supply you with templates and guidance for these focus groups and, by running these groups, we would both quickly see what fabrics, home furnishings, and fragrances might work.

Given our heritage, our fragrances all have, shall we say, a 'loamy fragrance', perhaps not suited for your population. Some of our home furnishings might work and, perhaps more aptly, there might be an interest in crafting our fabrics into clothing for Earthlings. What do you think?"

I reacted instantly. "I like your approach and agree with your assumptions. May I assume that we could license your technology for fabric color modification?"

"That's a tough one. We'll have to see which way the jabber dung falls."

Lingo handed me a note: "He means that we'd need to see how the relationship develops." I was glad to have Lingo around. Strange idioms!

Back to Xavier. "We took the liberty of crafting a strawman partnership agreement based on those previous assumptions. Why don't you show it to your attorneys and get back to us with any modifications? Our standard boilerplate terms and conditions form the bulk of the package."

And so, Xavier gave me a one hundred and sixty-three-page document to read at my leisure. I thanked Xavier and his team, gave Alice a hug, and went back to our Trigo.

On the way back to the hotel in Sheepla's Trigo, I asked if this visit might be typical of the ones scheduled in the ensuing days. Sheepla thought that it might be the case but advised that every enterprise culture was different and that we were in for some surprises.

Chapter 16: Baaweiser

Sheepla came to the hotel just after we finished breakfast. "Let's go, folks, we have a busy day today. We're going to try to fit in two stops today and, guess what? Our first stop is Baaweiser, the largest producer of Haykick on the planet. I'm hoping that they have some samples for us."

And we were off to Baaweiser. I was certain that I'd enjoy this Ohmy encounter.

Baaweiser's corporate offices were generic in nature, that is to say, that Baaweiser was housed in a shiny glass building just like all the other enterprises. The only difference I noticed as we entered the lobby was a large sign: "This Baa's for you!" We were met on our arrival, then taken to a conference room on the top floor marked "Board Room". A vice president did not greet us this time. Claudia.81.00.0012765, Director of Channel Marketing, was hosting us. She shuffled a stack of papers and then nervously addressed our little party:

"Hello, my name is Claudia.81.00.0012765. I'm from Baaweiser's corporate offices, in charge of channel marketing and I'm here to help. I work for Gilbert.81.00.020077, our Vice President of Marketing. Gilbert had to attend an emergency meeting this morning and could not host this session. He asked me to run with it. I'm sorry, but I'm ill prepared. Please tell me, once again, why you are here."

Another note from Lingo. "Run with it means you're on your own, Claudia."

Sheepla, the consummate professional, answered as tactfully as she could. "I contacted Gilbert recently to set up an exploratory meeting with Harry, our alien ambassador from Planet Earth. We'd like to see if a trade agreement with Earth is feasible. Perhaps, Claudia, you could start with an overview of Baaweiser and its products. We'll take it from there."

Claudia seemed somewhat relieved. "Alright then. Baaweiser is Baa's largest producer of Haykick. Our revenues are about one billion chips per year, and we have about two hundred Haykick sub-brands. We have millions of customers among the Baaners, the Ohmys, and even the Technobirds.

You may have read recently that we have gone through some cost-cutting measures to improve our profit picture. Simply put, 'we are drinking Haykick through a thin straw'."

(A note from Lingo: "She means that they cut her staff and she needs to work her butt off.")

"As a culture, we are maniacally focused on our customers. We believe strongly in test marketing and each sub-brand runs frequent customer satisfaction surveys.

I'm not sure if there is a good fit for our products on your planet. Haykick, as you may have noticed, is an acquired taste. Each sub-brand is carefully crafted from a different mixture of fermented grasses. You know what? Let me call downstairs for some samples. The best way to answer the feasibility question might be for you, Harry, to act as the official taster for your planet. What do you think?"

I knew that Clarence and Lingo would go for this idea, so I gave Claudia an emphatic "yes"!

After a quiet pause of a few minutes, two attendants came into the room, each pulling a cart full of hundreds of small sample-sized glasses of Haykick. The beverages ranged in color from pale amber to a deep rusty brown shade.

The attendants carefully arranged the samples on the conference table in a color shade sequence – light to dark.

Claudia passed around notebooks and pens. She then told us that we should read the small label on each glass, drink the shot of Haykick, and then write a comment in the notebook next to the page with the matching name. Very scientific.

Before we started, I noticed a big banner across the top of the Board Room's white board. It read: "Drink Responsibly!" Sheepla was driving, so I naturally assumed that the sign was meant for her – not for Clarence, Lingo and myself.

And so, we started: Grab a glass. Read the label. Find the page. Drink the sample. Write a comment. Etc. Etc,

After two hours of this rigorous exercise, I was unable to think clearly. I found that I was slurring my words and, to make things worse, a large wet spot had developed on my trousers. Had I had an accident? To hide the fact that it might be urine, I intentionally spilled the next sample on my lap. Claudia came over with a towel and started to rub my trousers, but I stopped her in progress and continued the wiping by myself. What an embarrassment! I whispered to Claudia that we had enough data for an informed decision and that we should bring the session to a natural conclusion.

"What do you think of our Haykicks?" Asked Claudia. "Tell me that you've enjoyed each one, that you've never had anything better tasting."

I thought I should be honest. "Perhaps I tried too many of your Haykick samples and maybe I need to review my notes, but, in truth, they all tasted the same!"

Claudia laughed. "Well, of course! This is for two reasons (1) Our cost-cutting measures and (2) We wanted the consistency of the product. As long as we have lots of choices in different colors, the customers are happy, and we crowd out the competition.

Before we conclude the meeting, Harry, I should mention that, should we decide to do business together, we'd gladly ship a team of our prized Prancing Jabbers to your planet. You've seen them in commercials, have you not?"

"No, Claudia, I'm afraid not. Might I be able to see them before we leave?"

Claudia was excited. "Certainly! We're about done here anyway. This is extraordinary timing; the next Prancing Jabbers commercial is being filmed right now in the back of our building. Let's go watch."

We walked around back and there they were – four heavyset jabbers harnessed to the front of a large float piled high with cases of Haykick. The jabbers were dressed up in pastel-colored finery, enhanced with silver bells. They were clearly not having a good time. Regardless, it was a sight to behold!

The background music started but the jabbers did not move forward; they just kind of hopped in place. I gave Claudia a puzzled look.

"This happens all the time, Harry. The float is too heavy for them. We just move the background up and down and run the video in slow-mo in sync with the music to give the appearance of forward motion. You'll love the commercial when you see it."

I told Claudia how much we enjoyed the filming of the Prancing Jabbers commercial, then wrapped up the meeting: "I thank you and your staff for a most informative session. I have taken copious notes and would like to review them in my hotel room. I'll get back to you through Sheepla should there be a good fit for your products."

At my urging, we postponed today's next meeting and went back to the hotel for a long nap. I needed to stop by Schnook Brothers to pick up my other two suits as this one was in need of a good cleaning.

Chapter 17: Poppyco and Lazy-Baa

The three musketeers, as I would like to call ourselves, were a little groggy and hung over the next morning. I told Clarence that I did not regard Baaweiser products as suitable for Earthlings. He laughed and agreed with me.

Our morning ritual continued with Sheepla picking us up after breakfast. "Good morning, once again! Today we're off to two enterprises: Poppyco and Lazy-Baa. Poppyco is Baa's largest supplier of non-alcoholic beverages and snack foods, while Lazy-Baa manufactures leisure furniture. I'm sure that you will find them to be educational and rewarding experiences."

Poppyco was a long drive from town. Their headquarters' complex was actually hidden in the woods an hour's drive from the hotel. We parked in the "Guest Area" and walked into the main lobby, adorned with walls of bright-colored product packaging – past and present.

The receptionist directed us to an auditorium on the main floor, where a large crowd awaited us. A friendly voice immediately greeted us:

"Hello, my name is Beatrice.81.00.005199. Welcome to Poppyco!

I am the Vice President of Marketing at Poppyco. I have invited my entire staff to sit in on this session. I'm hoping that the outcome of this will lead Poppyco into a new strategic direction.

I have a table with seating for all of us on the front stage. We have set up a microphone on the front table and the entire session is being recorded, with your permission of course! Please follow me."

I told Beatrice that recording the session would be fine with me, so we walked down one of the aisles while passing a wildly cheering mob of Ohmys. We ascended the stairs to the stage and took our places. I was certainly unprepared for this change of events!

The stage looked down on the Poppyco marketing staff. To the sides of the audience and in the back of us were large projection screens. A set of cameras was trained on us, showing our images on the projection screens.

Beatrice went into a flowery speech on how good it was to welcome me as an ambassador from Earth seeking trade relationships. I kept thinking "blah, baa, baa" as she spoke; she could have been any exec at any company. It did get more interesting when she discussed Poppyco's history.

"Two hundred years ago, the Poppyco founder decided that there was a market for a soothing beverage made from poppy seeds, a known narcotic. She experimented with thousands of mixtures of herbs and grasses, supplemented by 'sweetlah', the Baa equivalent of sugar. Finally, after years of taste testing, she had the desired result. She developed a proprietary method of extracting opiates from the poppy seeds and added small quantities of those opiates to the final product that was sold as a 'nerve tonic.' It was tasty, thirst quenching, and addictive. Given all of these attributes and a creative marketing campaign, the product 'Poppycola' became an instant success.

Over time, it became apparent that many of the Ohmys were in altered states and unable to perform their daily tasks. So, being responsible corporate citizens, we eliminated the opiates and boosted the sweetlah content. We now have over twenty varieties of Poppycola.

I should add that we've acquired a number of snack food companies. Salty snacks drive thirst and create a greater need for our beverage products."

Surprisingly, the conversation changed direction when Clarence commented. "I need to mention that the Baaners are considering legislation to limit the sweetlah content in beverages. There is also pending legislation to limit the size of beverage containers. Our population is becoming much more obese and our healthcare costs are rising dramatically. There have been many studies indicating a direct relationship between your products and the obesity levels, particularly in young lambs. Would you care to comment?"

Beatrice was startled at first. She then regained her composure. "This is true, Harry. We have heard rumors about the pending legislation. Our position on this topic has always been clear. We give our customers what they want, period. We would abide by any new rules and regulations, but I need to be clear on this – the responsibility for healthy decisions lies with the customer and not with Poppyco and certainly not with the government.

As it relates to the so-called studies to which Clarence refers, let me read to you a statement from our corporate physician:

'The studies correlating the consumption of sweetlah to obesity are fundamentally flawed for three reasons. (1) They were run on jabbers and not on Baaners, Technobirds or Ohmys. (2) Baaners do not exercise, have poor diets, and drink too much Haykick. Any studies against the Baaner population would, therefore, be unscientific. (3) The anti-sweetlah talk is just a fad. The real problem may be so called health foods or low-fat foods that are heavy in sweetlah content.

Look, I anticipated this turn of the conversation, so I have arranged an experiment."

Beatrice handed us each a tray containing a bowl of their salty snack products and three glasses marked 'A', 'B', and 'C'. "Here," she said. "Try a couple of snacks then drink the sample marked 'A', then repeat the process for 'B' and 'C'."

We did so. Beatrice then asked for a show of "hands" to indicate which beverage we liked the best. We all voted for 'C'.

Beatrice knew that she had the desired result. "Sample 'C' is always the winner.' Sample A' was low in sweetlah. Sample 'B' was our 'diet version' and 'Sample C' is high in sweetlah. This experiment clearly shows the relationship between salt and sweetlah."

The session lasted for another hour. Beatrice reiterated that their policy was always to give the customers what they wanted, even if what they wanted caused obesity or was addictive. Their world was a competitive world, after all.

I told Beatrice that the Earthlings had grappled with the obesity problem and slowly got away from the consumption of sweet non-alcoholic beverages and more towards drinking water. Beatrice even had an answer for that. She said that Poppyco had a new line of filtered drinking water and asked if those products would be of interest to me. I said that our planet had plenty of water but thanked her anyway.

On the way to our next stop, I asked Clarence if it might be a good idea to get on The Doctor Baz show for a substantive debate on the topic of sweetlah. Clarence said that he would set that up on our return from Corporus.

****

Lazy-Baa was actually a stop on our way back to the hotel. On the drive there, Sheepla explained that Lazy-Baa had once dominated the leisure furniture market but had fallen on hard times lately with inexpensive products being shipped in from other planets. She was not optimistic about a potential deal but said that they were anxious to meet with us.

... and anxious they were! As we pulled into the parking lot, BrookeSpiels.81.00.009222, the celebrity spokesperson for Lazy-Baa, met us and brought us into their showroom.

"We are all about comfort," said BrookeSpiels as she started her pitch. "Our recliners are made of the finest jabbercloth. Happy jabbers equals smooth jabbercloth – look at this..."

BrookeSpiels held up a framed picture of jabbers lounging in a grassy field. "See? The jabbers lounge around just waiting to provide their cloth to our happy customers. But don't take my word for it. Do come and try some recliners out."

The Lazy-Baa recliners seemed comfortable enough but were quite massive, perhaps being designed for the Ohmy market. With the urging from BrookeSpiels, I climbed into the recliner next to me. It was made from jabbercloth, of course, and was stained blue – my favorite color. There were control buttons on the side.

As I was just getting comfortable, BrookeSpiels came alongside and pushed one of the controls. The interior motor whirred, and the front part of the recliner slowly went down, leaving a growing gap in the center. Being smaller than those for whom the chair was designed, I fell unceremoniously into the growing gap with my butt jammed against the floor.

BrookeSpiels saw my plight and came to the rescue. She pushed another button that caused the entire recliner to fold up with me inside. I tried, to no avail, to wiggle free as Clarence and Lingo roared with laughter.

Sheepla was not amused. "This is a disaster, BrookeSpiels! Please get help immediately."

BrookeSpiels returned with two workers. They went into their toolboxes, took out the proper tools, and disassembled the recliner. I stepped out slowly, complaining of my back.

I took the time to thank an embarrassed BrookeSpiels for her time and got back into the Trigo. On the way back to the hotel we all agreed that we needed a break. A night on the town would do it nicely!

Chapter 18: Baaston Night Life

Even though my back still ached, I felt the need to spend an evening together with Sheepla, Clarence and Lingo. We agreed to meet in the lobby and then head out for dinner and drinks.

Sheepla said that we should eat at DuganPark, an old restaurant on the waterfront. She told us that it was informal, served traditional Baaston cuisine, and was known for its outspoken waitresses. She assured us that the food was good and that we'd have a few laughs.

We climbed the stairs to the second floor of the building and gave our name to the greeter. She promptly seated us at a "family style" table with an Ohmy tourist family. Our seats were wooden benches, somewhat uncomfortable for my aching back. Finally, our server arrived.

"Hello. My name is Colleen and I'll be your server. Have you been to DuganPark before? Is this your first visit to Baaston?" She eyed our little group. "And who is your jabber friend over there? Not that there's anything wrong with that."

Sheepla quickly came to my rescue. "He's no jabber. He's Harry from the Planet Earth. You'd better tone it down if you want a big tip."

Colleen probably knew that we'd give it right back to her. "Hey, can't you take a joke? Some of my best friends are jabbers. We serve jabbers all the time here. May I start you off with a drink while you look at our menu?"

Sheepla told us that she was going to pick up the tab, so she ordered Haykicks all around and asked us to study the menu. She recommended their house specials: jabbermeat pie, corn on the cob, and Baaston baked beans. She recommended their fruit pie topped with soy cheese for dessert.

After a few moments, Colleen returned with two large pitchers of Haykick and took our orders. On the way back to the kitchen she gave me a loving pat on my behind. I knew she meant no harm.

The family of Ohmys at the table had been watching us curiously. The father looked over at me... "So, you're from Earth, eh? I travel a great deal, but I've never been there. Is it like Baa? What brings you here anyway?

By the way, my name is Tony.81.00.005655. This is my wife Dotty.81.00.004488 and our lambson, Gerald. Good to meet you."

I told Tony that I was here on business, trying to set up trade relationships with some Ohmy enterprises. He seemed most interested in my endeavors and gave me his card. "Please contact me if you ever are in the market for insurance. I sell all kinds of insurance policies and annuities. You never know; you may need good insurance with all the traveling you do!"

So, I thanked Tony. Good grief, insurance salesmen are everywhere, even on Baa.

Colleen proudly strutted over with our dinners. I had to admit that everything was tasty. The jabbermeat pie was a little bit gamy so I did not have too much of that. On the other hand, the corn was sweet and delicious and the Baaston baked beans were the best I had ever had. I ordered two more bowls of baked beans, perhaps unaware of the potential consequences.

After Tony and his family left our table, we talked about our visits thus far, lessons learned, and the potential need to adjust our strategy. We concluded that every experience was a learning experience and that we should stay on course, as it were. I reminded Sheepla that the only potential deal making sense thus far was the one posed by RalphLawn for their fabric and color-modification technology. Although Sheepla was hoping for more, I think she fully understood.

We were sitting around drinking our Haykicks when Colleen came over with the dessert order. She probably wanted to make amends for her earlier faux pas, so she sat on the bench opposite me and asked me "Where are you off to now? You know there's a great bar around the corner. 'Shears'. You should check it out. They have a lively crowd and have a nightly "singsong" contest. I'm off work in an hour and I'll join you." (Sheepla described "singsong" to me later; it was just like Earth's "karaoke".)

Shears was a hubbub of activity. Dozens of raucous Ohmys gathered around a massive wooden bar, laughing and carrying on. We ordered a round of Haykicks and talked for a while. Then, the singsong started.

Sheepla urged me to get up on the stage and sing. She said that she would go first, but only if I'd follow. Feeling quite tipsy from the Haykicks and with a false sense of fearlessness, I volunteered.

Sheepla did a great job and was cheered heartily. Her first song was "The Wittlepoof Song":

"We're poor little lambs
Who have lost our way,
Baa Baa Baa,
We're little black sheep
Who have gone astray
Baa Baa Baa.

Ohmy songsters off on a spree
Doomed from here to eternity,
Holies, have mercy on such as we,
Baa Baa Baa."

Sheepla received a standing ovation and was asked to do an encore, this time with the whole crowd joining in the chorus.

Her second song was "Baabaa Ann":

"Tried Peggy Sue
Tried Betty Lou

Tried Mary Lou
But I knew she wouldn't do
Baabaa Ann, Baabaa Ann
Take my hand
Baabaa Ann
Take my hand
You got me rockin' and a-rollin'
Rockin' and a-reelin'
Baabaa Ann ba ba
Ba Baabaa Ann

Ba ba ba ba Baabaa Ann
Ba ba ba ba Baabaa Ann
Baabaa Ann Barbara Ann
Take my hand
Baabaa Ann
You got me rockin' and a-rollin'
Rockin' and a-reelin'
Baabaa Ann ba ba
Ba Baabaa Ann"

More applause and another standing ovation. Sheepla bowed to the crowd and then announced to me: "Thank you, thank you! Now for a real treat. I'd like you to give a hearty Baaston welcome to my friend Harry, from the Planet Earth!"

I walked up onto the stage. The crowd grew silent for a moment, stared at me, and then gave me a warm welcome.

As I walked across the stage, the beans and corn started to work on my system. I had to hold in the gas pressure; it was awful. Maybe I'd do one song and quit.

Obviously, they had no Earthling songs, so they played "Home on the pasture", a melancholy piece about their early days as primitive sheep roaming the pasture. An endearing song for the Ohmys and Baaners, less relevant for me!

I watched the last words on the display:

"... Where seldom is heard a discouraging word,
And we relish our days in the herd."

And then it happened: A succession of three loud blasts from the seat of my pants! As this was a soft, sweet song, the noise of my gaseous attack far outweighed the music. I did finish the song, but instead of applause, there was laughter and a great deal of it. Clarence, Lingo, and Sheepla were rolling on the floor in their mirth. How did I get roped into this?

As I came down the stairs, I was confronted by a leering Ohmy. "Hey, Jabber. Did you hear the joke about the jabber who went into a bar?

A jabber walks into a bar and says, 'A bottle of Haykick, please.' The jabber hands the bartender a ten-chip bill.

The bartender thinks to himself, 'This jabber doesn't know the price of drinks,' and gives no change.

The bartender says, 'You know, we don't get too many jabbers in here.'

The jabber replies, 'Well, at ten chips per drink, I ain't coming back, either.'

Pretty, funny, eh, jabs?"

I was somewhat offended but understood that this was just another drunken obnoxious Ohmy. Suddenly, Colleen, our server from the restaurant was standing at my side. She was not at all amused. "Leave my friend Harry alone!" she demanded. "Where are your manners anyway?"

With that, she repeatedly hit him over the head with her purse. "Be gone, idiot!" she yelled. And the buffoon left the bar with Colleen chasing after him.

Well, we did have our night on the town. I'd go back to the hotel to heal my pride and start my touring again tomorrow. Tomorrow, thankfully, was another day!

Chapter 19: Flipped Moss

Today's visit was to Flipped Moss, an enterprise specializing in what Sheepla called "recreational products", whatever that meant!

Flipped Moss was, once again, a bit of a drive from downtown Baaston. The Flipped Moss complex was down a long country road, surrounded by greenhouses and fields of multi-colored plants. Our liaison, Willy.81.00.017654, met us in the lobby and brought us into one of their many conference rooms. Willy did not have a prepared presentation; he much preferred an informal Q&A. He started the dialogue...

"Good morning. My name is Willy and I'm in charge of public relations here at Flipped Moss. I trust that Sheepla has briefed you on our products and marketing strategy?"

I replied that she had not and that we were in need of an overview.

"Very well, then. Flipped Moss started just over one hundred years ago. Back then, our only product was something called a 'weedette', a thin rolled-up paper tube filled with a plant called 'weedacco'. One would ignite the tube, put it in one's mouth, and then inhale the fumes. The fumes, in turn, gave our customers a sense of exhilaration – hence the term 'recreational product'. Weedettes were immensely popular with males, and then, after successful marketing campaigns, they became a hit with females and lambs. May I demonstrate?"

I replied that it would not be necessary and that we had similar products years ago on my planet. I did not mention anything about the years of controversy – I'd wait to see what Willy had to say first.

Willy continued. "We recognized that we needed variations of the main product for our different market segments. Our flagship brand was 'Machoboro' and was targeted to the male Ohmys, Technobirds, and Baaners. We then created fifteen weedette brands, including 'Ginny Slims' for females, 'Spiderweed' for lambs, and 'Weedsafe', a filtered product for anyone excessively health conscious. Finally, we invested in 'Filler High Life', a brewer of Haykick, feeling that Haykick is a natural complement to weedettes. Won't you please try out one of our weedettes? I'm sure you'll enjoy it!"

With that Henrietta, Willy's assistant brought out a tray containing packs of ten of the weedette brands. She also brought ashtrays and glasses of 'Filler Light' Haykick. Being brave, I lit up a Machoboro weedette.

I would describe the taste and the smell of the fumes as 'acrid', but not totally unpleasant. I felt nothing at first but, as I neared the end of the weedette, I vacillated between a sense of euphoria and a feeling of paranoia. Maybe the weedette I chose was too strong for me. Maybe it was designed for a creature much larger than I, a male Ohmy for instance. I squirmed in my seat. I wanted the euphoria to continue and I wanted the paranoia to fade away. I'd better not have another one!

"What do you think?" asked Willy. "Pretty good, eh?"

I turned to Clarence. "This stuff's pretty good. Is it legal across the board? For small lambs, for instance?"

Clarence put his Machoboro out in his ashtray. "Sure. Weedettes are perfectly legal for any Baaner age group. The lambs really go for Spiderweed in a big way.

Did I tell you that Flipped Moss and I have been working together for many years? They are my largest campaign contributor."

The picture was becoming clearer now. This situation was analogous to an earlier era on Earth when we weighed the health concerns about marijuana and tobacco against the potential health risks. Just then it occurred to me that weedacco was actually a cross between tobacco and marijuana. No wonder!

The Earth's history of the tobacco industry and the marijuana industry flashed before me. I'd need to ask more questions: "And tell me, Willy, are your products as successful with the Ohmys and Technobirds?"

"Of course!" said Willy proudly. "Why shouldn't they be?"

"Interesting. On our planet, we used to produce similar products. 'Tobacco' contained a drug called 'nicotine' and was proven to have carcinogenic properties. We required the producers of tobacco-related products to post warnings about health hazards. We kept raising the taxes on these products until they became prohibitively expensive.

We also had something called 'marijuana' that was smoked in a manner more like your weedacco. Marijuana had an interesting history. At first, it was outlawed, and then it slowly became permitted for medicinal purposes. Finally, it became a successful commercial offering, but only for adults. We did find that it had a negative impact on children while their brains were being formed.

What is your reaction to this? I take it that the legislation is laxer on Baa."

"Indeed yes," answered Willy. "We view ourselves as intelligent creatures, able to weigh the benefits against the risks. Look, there are risks in everything from weedacco to Haykick to so called health foods. We understand these risks and we make our choices."

"But what about the lambs? Are they wise enough to make those choices?"

"No. But their parents are. We have a range of product offerings you know. Spiderweed is a 'lite' version specifically designed for lambs. We have a lite Haykick for young lambs. We're just now introducing 'Electronic Spiderweed' for young lambs, and a line of weedacco derivatives for physicians and hospitals.

Look, Harry. Take this box of samples back to Earth with you. I'm sure your fellow Earthlings will enjoy our suite of products and want you to set up a distribution channel."

I figured a way out of this... "But there's this problem. The Galactic Shuttle that will take me home has strict regulations about what I can take onboard. I'm sure that the security agents would confiscate your samples. They might even put me in jail.

Let me take your suggestions under advisement. I'll get back to you through Sheepla if there is any further interest."

We were about to leave when Clarence asked Willy if he could bring several sample boxes back to his congressional constituents, knowing full well that we would consume them long before then – perhaps in the solitude of our hotel rooms.

Chapter 20: Baattel and Woolmart

As we were driving to our next two destinations, Sheepla gave us a quick preview... "Our first stop is Baattel, the largest manufacturer of toys on all of Baa. Then, after lunch, we'll meet with SamWoolton, the founder and owner of Woolmart, our largest retailer. It will be a long day, but I think you'll be interested in what they both have to say."

Toys? Maybe there might be a fit. I wasn't so sure about Woolmart though. We certainly had enough major retailers back on Earth. We'd have to see what SamWoolton had up his sleeve.

The Baattel presentation was ultra-high tech. The presentation was done remotely by Holovision and led by the Vice President of Marketing, Justin.81.00.03543. One after another, a Baattel product manager would appear on Holovision before us and discuss his or her product offering(s). The first presenter was their head of Fishy Priced Toys, a Baattel subsidiary. She discussed a wide variety of toys, most of them wooden and all of them made inexpensively on other planets. The toys were obviously targeted for different customer segments. They had wooden farmhouses, farm workers and pull-toy jabbers for the Baaners. They had miniature corporate headquarters, with toy CEOs, CIOs, CFOs, COOs, and lawyers for the young Ohmys. They even had "bobble head" pull-toys of Bill.77.00.000018 for the Technobirds. Very creative, but probably not for our Earthling population.

Reminded of earlier controversies on Planet Earth, I asked if there were sufficient quality controls because we had instances when excessive amounts of lead paint were found when the manufacture of our toys was remotely outsourced. Once again, I was assured that Baattel took this very seriously and that random samples of each toy were given to a team of jabbers to chew on, testing for ill effects.

The second presenter was in charge of their board game division. Their most successful product offering was their "Life Series". Once again clever with their target marketing, they had board games simulating, for the young lambs, the "life process" in various demographic segments. They had, for instance:

"Life on the Farm" for the Baaners
"Life in Congress" for the Bigbeards
"Life in the Monastery" for the Blacknecks
"Life with the Intelligencia" for the Knowbies
"Life on a Linear Family Tree" for the Rednecks
"Life for the Insignificant" for the "33s"
"Life with the Homeless" for the "51s"
"Life" for the "00s"
"Life for the Holier-Than-Thou" for the Lumens
"Life working with Bill" for the Technobirds
"Life on the Corporate Ladder" for the Ohmys

I told the product manager for the board games that some of these might have direct applicability on Earth, "Life in Congress", for instance.

The third presenter was in charge of video games. These games were the interactive versions of the "Life" games we had just witnessed. The video formats on Baa were so vastly different than our formats that I quickly dismissed the presenter, not wishing to waste his time.

For the grand finale, Justin elected to do the presentation himself.

"We intentionally left the best for last," exclaimed Justin. "Perhaps you've heard of our famous 'Baabee Doll' line of toys? Well, we've added many technological enhancements and we've vastly increased the size of our repertoire. What I'd like to do is summarize the technology modifications and then use Holovision to show you representative samples.

We've always had an audio playback capability. You've always been able to touch parts of the doll and elicit an appropriate canned response. Now, what we've added is this: You can actually record your voice and tie that recording to a touch sensation on the doll's body. Tickle her feet and have her say 'tee hee', for instance.

But wait, there's more! We have inflatable Baabee Dolls in many sizes and in many varieties. These inflatable dolls have carefully crafted and realistic body parts.

And there's more! We have Baabee Doll interactive videos in which you can interact personally with a Baabee Doll of your choice.

Last but not least: Edible Baabee Dolls in a choice of five flavors!

What do you think, Harry?"

My initial thoughts were far too risqué for these, my memoirs. I needed some time for a thoughtful response, so I said "Interesting. Most interesting. I'd prefer to see the representative samples if you don't mind..."

Justin continued. "Well, on with the show!"

The first holographic image was a demonstration of audio programming. A young female Ohmy removed the Baabee Doll's dress and undergarments, exposing her buttocks. She then flipped open the left buttock to reveal a panel. She pressed a button on the panel, spoke into the doll's left cheek while recording 'I love you', then pushed another button and closed the panel.

Then, she flipped open a panel on the right buttock, revealing a long wire that she used to touch the mouth of the doll. She then closed the panel and said, 'watch this!'

When she kissed the Baabee Doll on the lips, it said 'I love you'. I was left speechless. After a moment or two of dead silence, Clarence, Lingo and I gave our polite applause.

The second demonstrator appeared as the first disappeared into the ether. He was at the controls of a video game console. An image of a miniature Baabee Doll appeared in an Ohmy-sized kitchen, with a sink piled high with dishes. Using the controls, the demonstrator moved the tiny Baabee into the sink with the dishes, putting her to work scrubbing each and every dish.

Lingo, the truth be known, had a dark sense of humor. Turning to Justin, he interrupted the demonstration: "Put her in the blender!"

"What?" said Justin? "You're not serious?"

"I am indeed. I want to be sure that this is a live demonstration and not a canned one that was slapped together just for us. Please put her in the blender."

Justin contacted the demonstrator who then manipulated the controls to position the Baabee Doll over the blender. With a flip of a switch and a touch of the button, she was in the blender set on "high". Let us just say that the demonstration was successful. Shame on Lingo, but he did make his point. Justin asked meekly "May we continue?"

Next came a demonstrator with the parade of inflatable Baabee Dolls. They came as either male or female. They were in three styles: Ohmy adult and child, Baaner adult and child, and Technobird. The attention to detail was remarkable; they were almost like wax museum replicas.

Justin took charge of the presentation once again. "I mentioned that there are five flavors of edible Baabee Dolls. There are four fruit flavors and one chocolate. Here is a sample of the chocolate..."

With that, Justin passed out small chunks of a Barbee Doll's leg, chocolate in flavor. We all took a bite and commented on the quality of the chocolate.

Justin saw that we were pleased with his presentation. He continued... "Watch this now. Here is a rolling list of the many current varieties of Baabee Dolls."

He dimmed the lights and pointed to a large screen where we saw, in slow succession:

Baaner (lamb, ewe, ram)
Ohmy (lamb, ewe, ram)
Technobird (ewe, ram)
Recording option
Inflatable option
Edible option
Custom (if quantity order)

Clarence had to ask the next question. "And what custom Baabee Dolls have you done? Please give some examples."

Justin paced around while he thought of the best custom dolls. "OK, Clarence. We did one for the NewBaa Rifle Association; she was in fatigues and carrying a laser ray gun. We did a pregnant Baabee for the Baa Mothers' Club. Then there was a 'Trailer Trash Baabee', a 'Saloon Baabee' and an inflatable 'Tattoo Baabee' for the Rednecks. The Tattoo Baabee was a failure because it deflated once a new tattoo was applied. Oh yes, we also did a pious Baabee for the Blacknecks.

I should mention also some niche market Baabee Dolls that had limited success: An edible Baabee on a bun, a frozen Baabee on a stick, a jabber Baabee, a homeless Baabee with a shopping cart, a roadkill Baabee and a diarrhea Baabee. In trying to inject Baabee into some real-life situations, we obviously had a few bad ideas."

We all laughed. Recalling some earlier problems with Earth's Barbie Dolls, I wanted to ask Justin a few questions. "Was there any feedback from your customers about the Baabee character having an unrealistically optimized figure? Being a little too perfect as it were?"

"Yes. We had some complaints. Actually, there was a period of time when envious teenage ewes were decapitating their Baabee Dolls. Those issues seemed to dissipate somewhat as we added new features and functions."

Clarence added to the discussion. "True; I had been aware of those developments. I had also heard reports of some religious Lumen and Blackneck Baaners being highly offended. They actually started a petition to ban inflatable Baabees."

Justin tried to wrap things up. "We've shown you some of our many products, Harry. Do you think any of our product offerings would be successful on your planet?"

I said that I needed to review my many pages of notes and that I'd get back to him.

On the way back to Sheepla's Trigo, we stopped in the Baabee Store. Clarence and Lingo each ordered an inflatable Baabee. They blew them up and had them sit next to them on the ride to Woolmart.

****

We stopped at a local restaurant for lunch, leaving the two inflatable Baabees sitting in the Trigo. The luncheon conversation took an unexpected turn when Sheepla confided in us.

"I'm really enjoying your company; no joke. I have to confess that my normal office routine is oppressive and it's good to be out with friends."

Her beautiful black eyes were welling with tears. "Why, what's the matter, Sheepla?", I asked.

"It's my boss. He keeps trying to, you know, with me. I can't get any work done. It's affecting my job performance."

Clarence piped in. "But I thought sex in the workplace was common and consensual?

"You're so wrong, Clarence." Sheepla quickly replied. "It is consensual from time to time, but it is a major obstacle if you are career minded and find that it gets in the way of your job performance. I'm just not interested in sex. I want to get ahead but have trouble saying 'no' to my boss." She burst into tears.

Clarence had a thoughtful response. "Here is my card. Call me and I'll introduce you to Taranabaa.81.00.0053667. She started the 'Ewetoo Movement' and will advise you on how to handle your office dilemma."

Sheepla took Clarence's card, gave him a big hug, and went back to being her classy efficient self.

****

A lunch, Sheepla drove the short distance to Woolmart headquarters. SamWoolton's personal assistant was waiting for us in the lobby. She then escorted us to Sam's spacious penthouse office.

Sam greeted us from behind his hand-carved wooden desk. "Good afternoon and welcome to Woolmart. As you know, Woolmart is a family-owned retailer. We are the largest retail operation on all of Baa with over ten thousand stores.

Sheepla has informed me that you might be open to considering Woolmart franchise operations on Planet Earth. Did I get that correctly?"

I nodded my head. "That is correct, Sam. I told Sheepla that I wasn't sure that Woolmart would be a good fit because of the many retailers we currently have back on Earth. Sheepla said that we should still meet with you to hear your story. How do you differentiate yourselves from a competitive standpoint?"

"Economy of scale and cheap labor. Because of our massive size, we can purchase products less expensively and pass those savings on to our customers. We also pay our workers minimum wages or less to keep our costs down. Lower costs help us to keep our low-price points."

Clarence obviously knew more about their cost-cutting tactics. "I'd like to put my two chips in. Is it not also true that your working conditions are spartan at best? That your healthcare benefits are minimal? And would you kindly address why Woolmart is a factor in our income inequality issues?"

Retaining his composure, Sam had an immediate response. "That used to be the case. We have made substantial improvements since then.

Look, Clarence. We are the largest employer on all of Baa. We hire from among the disadvantaged: the '00s', the '33s' and even the '51s'. Where would they find employment if not for us? They get opportunities that they would never have otherwise; they are happy with the wage structure such as we have it. Have you not seen the statistics which show we actually have a significant impact on the overall unemployment rate?

You should know, Clarence, that income inequality is a natural outgrowth of our capitalistic system. I get paid millions of chips annually but I'm worth millions of chips annually. It's simply survival of the fittest. Any smart and aggressive Ohmy can rise to the top like me. As it relates to the disadvantaged, I've already stated our position: We take care of them."

I had to voice my concerns also. "If you were to bring one of your mega-stores into one of our towns would it not create unfair competition for our local 'mom and pop' merchants? Would the local politicians not be influenced by those local merchants and block you?"

Sam had an answer for that too. "Your local merchants probably charge outrageous prices for their merchandise. Putting them out of business is a good thing for the town's consumers."

And Clarence added: "That may be true. You also bribe the local politicians into passing rulings on your local stores."

I felt bad for Sam and wanted to defuse any ill will. "I'd be very interested in reading a detailed business plan for our planet. Please include your ideas for product sources and labor sources. If you were to sell only our earthly goods, you'd have a major expenditure in learning our culture and our products. If you sold only Baa's products, there may not be a sufficient market for those items back on Earth. Please address those concerns and send your proposal to my hotel."

Sam agreed with my suggested next steps. We thanked him for his time and headed back to Baaston and our hotel. The ride back was uncomfortable, being squeezed next to the inflatable Baabee Dolls, but at least we bypassed all of the stopped traffic by using the high occupancy lane. We figured the police would not stop us since the Baabee Dolls were so lifelike.

Chapter 21: Deep Sheep

Clarence and Lingo left their inflatable Baabees in the hotel room. Sheepla picked us up again in the lobby and we were off to meet with the Research Division of Intergalactic Business Systems (IBS). As we were on our way, an excited Sheepla said that we would "love this one".

Sheepla's Trigo ascended a steep hill within a quiet wooded area. When we reached the pinnacle, we drove down a long driveway and parked in front of a magnificent pyramidal glass structure, the home of IBS Research.

No sooner did we enter the lobby when we were greeted by a distinguished looking Ohmy, dressed in a fine charcoal-gray suit, topped with a white lab coat. "Good morning! My name is Alexander.81.00.028765 and I'll be your tour guide today. Please follow me; I have reserved our Executive Demonstration Room."

As we tagged along behind Alexander, Sheepla whispered that our host had won a number of prestigious awards for technology innovation and that we were most lucky to have him as our guide!

The conference room seated well over three hundred Ohmys, so we rattled around – just the four of us in the front row. Pointing to a large screen behind a stage brimming with electronics, Alexander started his presentation. "I'd like to give you an overview of IBS and its history, show you 'Deep Sheep', our flagship Artificial Intelligence product, and then demonstrate our 'Electric Sheep' robotics technology. All of this should take us to our lunch break, during which we'll discuss your specific requirements on Planet Earth. Does this sound like a plan?"

We nodded to show our concurrence, and then Alexander started. "IBS began over a hundred years ago, producing manual typewriters. We then moved into electric typewriters and early/primitive computers. Our first computers were large vacuum tube devices, far less powerful than the computers we now have in small wristwatch form.

As our name implies, IBS serves mainly business customers. We dabble in the consumer space every once in a while, but our strength lies in producing solutions for medium-to-large enterprises.

We are the second-largest employer in all of Baa. Our annual revenues exceed one hundred billion chips and we are highly profitable.

This, our Research Division, has received almost one thousand prestigious awards. We have patents for everything from cash registers, barcodes, and ATMs to supercomputers."

Alexander went on for another fifteen minutes before getting to the topic of "Deep Sheep". "Ten years ago, we were put in contact with Trayback.81.00.027885, the host of 'Wager', the famous Holovision show in which contestants bet large amounts of chips if they think they might know the question for which there is an answer in a predetermined category. Trayback wanted to know if any of our computers could compete with some of their top contestants. We told Trayback that, yes, we thought that our computers might have a chance on his show, but we'd need more time.

What we did then was to feed all of the news articles from the last ten years into 'Deep Sheep', our supercomputer. We then added our proprietary natural language interface to the system and, voila, we were ready for Trayback.

We were nervous when the 'Wager' show started, but that anxiety quickly vanished as Deep Sheep showed its true colors. We handily beat Wager's top contestants.

Since then, we have put Deep Sheep to work for many customers: doing medical diagnoses, predicting stock market behavior, and parsing interplanetary chatter to look for invasion threats.

Now, without further ado, we present 'Deep Sheep'!"

Alexander pointed to the enormous array of flashing lights on the stage. I was impressed but had no idea what I should do next. There was nothing but silence and flashing lights.

After a few tense moments, Alexander passed his microphone over to me... "Here, Harry. Give Deep Sheep an answer, any answer."

I scratched my head, deep in thought, and then I spoke into the microphone. "Jabbers."

Deep Sheep responded, "Please state your category."

"Baa"

"Baa is not a valid category; try again."

Alexander gave me a book of valid categories. I skimmed it quickly.

"Planet Baa"

"Please restate your answer for Planet Baa."

"They are called Jabbers!"

"What are primitive ape-like creatures?"

I was blown away! Looking at the category list, I thought I'd try another answer. "Category is 'pop culture'. The answer is the Queen of pop culture."

"Who is Lady Baabaa?"

Of course, I had no way of knowing if Deep Sheep was correct, but I kept giving answers anyway.

The "answering" process continued for a few more minutes, after which Alexander took the stage again. "As Sheepla may have told you, IBS Research is experimenting with sophisticated robotics technology. Paying homage to our primitive sheep-like ancestors, we call our line of experimental robots 'Electric Sheep'.

The way that we program Electric Sheep to do a specific task is this... First, we whisper the task's name into the ear of the robot, and then we press the 'learn' button on the robot's head. The Ohmy instructing the robot then wears wireless gloves and wireless slippers that continually transmit behavior instructions to the robot. Whatever the instructor does, the robot will mimic. Now watch!"

An instructor, again wearing a white lab coat but also equipped with iridescent yellow gloves and slippers entered the room. He was wheeling in a sheep-like robot about seven hoofs tall. The robot had two arms and two legs and was wearing the same yellow gloves and slippers.

"Good morning!" said the instructor. "My name is Henry.81.00.0138564 and this is 'Jessica'. I am going to train Jessica to serve all of you drinks of grassade."

Henry wheeled Jessica to the center of the stage. He then gave us each an empty glass to hold. While we held our glasses, he whispered "grassade" in Jessica's ear and hit Jessica's "learn" button, activating learning mode. Henry then obtained a full pitcher of grassade from a table on the stage and walked down a ramp to the first row where we all were seated. He poured a full glass of grassade into each of our glasses and went back to the stage, placing the pitcher back onto the table.

A classic drama then ensued. Henry yelled across the room "Jessica: grassade" and Jessica went into motion. She rolled over to the table, picked up the pitcher, went down the ramp and poured each of us another glass of grassade. Regrettably, our glasses were not yet empty, so some minor spillage did occur.

As we applauded, however, Henry was paged and had to leave the room. Jessica knew that she had her job to do. She went back to the stage, placed the pitcher on the table, picked up the pitcher and returned down the ramp to serve us more grassade. This time, the spillage was substantial: we all had soaking wet pants.

Embarrassed, I asked Alexander if we might terminate the demonstration. Alexander was quite distressed, saying, "I don't know how!"

I suggested to Alexander that we'd best get back to the hotel and change our clothing, so we started out of the room with Jessica following – pitcher in hand. We went into the lobby and so did Jessica. We got into the Trigo, but Jessica was right behind, knocking on the door.

Sheepla hit the methane pedal and we were quickly in transit, knocking over poor Jessica in the parking lot. Do you remember Paul Dukas' Sorcerer's Apprentice music? I couldn't help recalling the ancient movie "Fantasia" with Mickey Mouse and the brooms carrying buckets of water.

We went back to the hotel for a change of clothes. That night I had the weirdest dream: I was lying in bed when Jessica kept storming into my hotel room with large pitchers of Haykick, one after another. She kept coming up to the bed and pouring Haykick into my open mouth. It was awful! I couldn't breathe and woke up in a cold sweat. It could have been worse, I suppose.

Chapter 22: Hormal and Lady Baabaa

When we entered the lobby the next morning, there was a message awaiting me from Frederick.81.00.001976, Lady Baabaa's agent. It read:

"We are scheduling a recording session at Overbuzz Studios this evening; will you be able to join us? Perhaps Sheepla, Clarence and Lingo would care to come along? Please call me."

Sheepla came into the lobby and we had a discussion about the note from Frederick and the activities we had planned for the day. We all thought Frederick's note was exciting and that we should not pass up the opportunity. However, thrilling the note, it was also ambiguous: Did Lady Baabaa want Sheepla, Clarence, and Lingo to just sit in on the recording session? Or did they want them as a vocal accompaniment? We were not sure. Just then Lingo had a fabulous idea...

"Let's assume that Lady Baabaa did want us to join in the recording process. I can't carry a tune. I don't think Clarence can and Sheepla's voice was still hoarse from the other night at Shears. Why don't we call Frederick back and tell him we'll meet them at the studio after dinner? We should also ask Alexander at IBS if we could borrow a few of their 'Electric Sheep' for the chorus. Think of the publicity it could bring IBS!"

Clarence made the arrangements. We would make our morning call at Hormal Foods, a processed food supplier, then stop at IBS to sign an agreement and pick up three Electric Sheep. We'd have our dinner then set off for Overbuzz Studios.

****

After we checked into the lobby of Hormal Foods, we were escorted to a small second floor meeting room that overlooked their food processing plant. After doing our introductions, Polly.81.00.015223 led the Hormal presentation.

"Hello. My name is Polly.81.00.015223 and I am Hormal's Vice President of Marketing. I'd like to give you a quick overview of Hormal and then show you our brand-new food processing plant in actual operation. I'd like to keep this session informal, so please ask questions at any point in time."

Polly went over to power up the computer that was to give the presentation. The large projection screen flashed momentarily then revealed a light blue background with the cryptic message "0xc0000225; please reboot".

Polly was furious. "Those jabbers over at Mesa View! They can't do anything right. Please bear with me while I reboot."

And so, she rebooted. This time the presentation loaded properly, much to Polly's delight.

"As you can see, we've been in the food processing business for over one hundred years. Most of our products are made from processed jabber meat, as you'll see momentarily. Recently, however, we took over "Sticky Peanut Butter", the second largest producer of peanut butter on Baa. We also sell ready-to-roast jabber parts under the name "Jabby-O".

Our main processed jabber products are "Wonderful Weenies" and "Spum". Perhaps you've heard of them? Here are some samples to try out.

Polly brought over a tray of samples Wonderful Weenies and some Spum on toast. We all took a bite of each. Personally, I thought the weenies and Spum tasted about the same – quite salty and more than a subtle hint of garlic. I bolted down Polly's appetizers and let her continue...

"We take great pride in our patented six-step process.

Step 1: The jabbers are humanely terminated. A quick electric shot to the head.

Step 2: All of the body hair is removed using our patented electrostatic process. The jabber hair is sent away as material for sweaters.

Step 3: A team of robots cut out the sections most desirable for roasting. They go to Jabby-O for packaging and shipment.

Step 4: The remaining parts: skull, bones, brains, feet, hands, and viscera are put into our chopper.

Step 5: Preservatives are added to the chopper.

Step 6: Output from the chopper goes in four separate directions:

One stream of jabber output goes into casements for our sausage products.

A second stream is canned as "Spum".

The third stream is dried and bagged as fertilizer.

The fourth stream is dyed pink and sold as a meat supplement.

So that's how we process jabbers into our fine foods. We do not waste any part of the jabber and take pride in our efficiency.

Let's go downstairs now for our tour of the plant. Any questions first?"

I did have one question: "The Earthlings discovered many years ago that there was a direct correlation between food additives and cancer. Have you had such studies on Baa? Have you seen any health-related issues stemming from your use of preservatives?"

Polly was quick to respond. "Yes, we have. That's why we put a small percentage of our profits into cancer research. That building over there (pointing) is the Hormal Cancer Research Institute."

Polly had not noticed that I was turning a pale green during her talk. She did notice, however, when I heaved my breakfast into her tray of weenie and Spum samples.

Sheepla came to the rescue. "I'm sorry, Polly, but we need to get Harry to a doctor. He must have a stomach virus of some sort. We will call you soon to reschedule your plant tour."

Of course, we would not! Clarence and Lingo had seen and heard enough too. I wiped my face carefully with one of Polly's napkins and we were off again.

****

We stopped to rent a trailer on the way to IBS Research; there would have been no room for the Electric Sheep otherwise. Alexander was waiting for us when we pulled up to one of the loading docks. We signed a sheath of release papers and were about to leave, Electric Sheep in tow when Alexander offered to send one of his assistants along to help. We declined, saying that we'd be up late that night and that there might not be enough room in Lady Baabaa's studio.

When we arrived at the studio, we were quickly admitted to the main recording wing. I wheeled in one of the Electric Sheep, as did both Clarence and Lingo.

Lady Baabaa came out from the dressing room to meet us. She gave us each a big hug and kiss then looked quizzically at our prizes from IBS. She burst out laughing!

"What in the world are these? Do they have a union card?" Said Lady jokingly. "You must be kidding!"

I explained that these were experimental programmable robots from IBS. I said that Lingo's idea was to have them programmed to sing a chorus in one or two of her songs.

Lady Baabaa got the idea immediately. "Brilliant! Brilliant!" "We are going to do one major song tonight, one called "Baahemian Rhapsody". Here are the words:"

She handed us the lyrics:

"Is this the real life?
Is this just fantasy?
Caught in a landslide,
No escape from reality.

Open your eyes,
Look up to the skies and see,
I'm just a poor ewe, I need no sympathy,
Because I'm easy come, easy go,
Little high, little low,
Anyway the wind blows doesn't really matter to me, to me.

Mama, just killed a ram,
Put a gun against his head,
Pulled my trigger, now he's dead.
Mama, life had just begun,
But now I've gone and thrown it all away.

Mama, ooh,
Didn't mean to make you cry,
If I'm not back again this time tomorrow,
Carry on, carry on as if nothing really matters.

Too late, my time has come,
Sent shivers down my spine,
Body's aching all the time.
Goodbye, everybody, I've got to go,
Gotta leave you all behind and face the truth.

Mama, ooh (anyway the wind blows),
I don't wanna die,
I sometimes wish I'd never been born at all.

I see a little silhouetto of a ram,
Scaramouche, Scaramouche, will you do the Fandango?
Thunderbolt and lightning,
Very, very frightening me.
(Galileo) Galileo.
(Galileo) Galileo,
Galileo Figaro
Magnifico.

I'm just a poor ewe, nobody loves me.
She's just a poor ewe from a poor family,

Spare her her life from this monstrosity.

Easy come, easy go, will you let me go?
Bismillah! No, we will not let you go. (Let her go!)
Bismillah! We will not let you go. (Let her go!)
Bismillah! We will not let you go. (Let me go!)
Will not let you go. (Let me go!)
Never, never let you go
Never let me go, oh.
No, no, no, no, no, no, no.
Oh, mama mia, mama mia (Mama mia, let me go.)
Beelzebub has a devil put aside for me, for me, for me.

So you think you can stone me and spit in my eye?
So you think you can love me and leave me to die?
Oh, baby, can't do this to me, baby,
Just gotta get out, just gotta get right outta here.

(Oh, yeah, oh yeah)

Nothing really matters,
Anyone can see,
Nothing really matters,
Nothing really matters to me.

Anyway the wind blows."

"So, here's the plan," said Lady, "Harry and I will start the song up to the 'Mama I just killed a ram' line. Then I'll do a solo until 'I see a little silhouetto of a ram' at which point Harry and the Electric Sheep will come in. The sheep will shuffle back and forth and chime in with the '(Galileo) Galileo' verse. I'll wind up the song with another solo part. Got it?"

I had been writing notes furiously. I went over my notes a few times with Frederick and we were almost ready for show time. While the studio was getting ready, I slipped into the IBS yellow gloves and slippers and taught the Electric Sheep how to shuffle back and forth on their wheels (Program #1). The next Program (#2) was more difficult – teaching them to shuffle while singing the Galileo chorus. Oh yes, by the way – Alexander showed us how to use the program stop button, so we'd not have a repeat of the infamous grassade incident.

As you might expect, the first two takes were unsuccessful. On take #1, one of the Electric Sheep shuffled off of the stage, knocking over one of the stagehands. On Take #2, Lady Baabaa didn't like how I used my voice for the Electric Sheep; I had to reprogram the sheep with her voice.

The third take was a huge success. Frederick told us that the song was recorded in both audio and Holovision formats and would be available for purchase next week.

We all went over to Shears to wind up the evening with many rounds of Haykick. What a day!

Chapter 23: Wow Chemicals

Sheepla did not think that today's visit to Wow Chemicals would be fruitful, but she felt it was necessarily a part of our doing "our homework". According to Sheepla, Wow Chemicals was the largest producer of chemical-related products on all of Baa. Chemicals, genetic modifications, waste management – they did it all. Interesting, yes. But applicability to Earthlings? Maybe.

Wow Chemicals headquarters were a good distance away from Baaston. It took us most of the morning to get there. Once again, we went through the ritual of being met in the lobby and escorted to a multimedia conference room.

Carla.81.00.017768 gave us a warm greeting. She was Director of Channel Sales. "Good Morning. Welcome to Wow Chemicals. I have a short presentation for you. We'll have some lunch, and then I'll take you on a brief tour. I'd appreciate it if you'd ask questions as we go along. Is this an acceptable agenda?"

We nodded our heads affirmatively, and then Carla continued by showing a multimedia presentation. "Wow Chemicals is involved with all of the governments on Baa. I'm sure that you have been told that we contribute heavily to Baa's tax coffers. You may not have known, however, that we have large governmental contracts."

We were treated to a Holovision image of a nuclear explosion. It was as if the room around us was filled with the heat and radiation of a nuclear blast! I just about jumped out of my seat.

"Fifty years ago, when nuclear weapons were in vogue, we managed the government nuclear test sites. This experience gave us the knowledge to manage the removal of nuclear waste, which we now do, Baa-wide, in all nuclear power facilities."

I was curious about a few things, so I interrupted Carla... "I did not know that nuclear power was used on Baa. I thought all of the energy sources were methane-based. How many power plants are there and how do you dispose of the waste?"

"There are over three hundred operational nuclear power plants on Baa. As far as the waste disposal procedure goes, we process the raw waste to create some of our plant food additives, the rest is put into iron canisters and buried deep in the ground on Nowhereland. We used to dump the canisters in the ocean, but we later discovered that the iron enclosures were rusting, posing a danger to sea life."

"And have there been no ill effects on Nowhereland?"

"There have been rumors of some mutations near the dumpsite – Baaners with multiple heads, etc. We have yet to verify these rumors and do scientific case studies, but who cares? The Nowhereland inhabitants are scum, after all.

Moving right along... Another key business area, partially subsidized by our governments, is genetic modification. Did you know that the Technobirds and the Ohmys are the results of genetic modifications within our facilities?"

"Yes," I answered. "I did know about those experiments, but I did not know that Wow scientists were involved. While we're on that topic, please explain why Baaners are in the '76' gene pool while Technobirds are '77s' and Ohmys are '81s'. Why is there a gap between '77' and '81'?"

Carla seemed embarrassed. "That's the 64,000-chip question. The Ohmys came about as the result of genetic changes to the pituitary glands. There were three 'throw away' species that were introduced before the Ohmys were successfully created. The '78s' had Baaner-sized bodies and enormous heads; they kept toppling over. We shipped them to Nowhereland. They may still be there, as far as I know.

The next experiments led to the creation of the '79s'. These unfortunate creatures were no taller than one hoof. We thought of keeping them around to do useful chores for us, like acting as doorstops. They got underfoot, however, and died out after being inadvertently squashed.

The next species we created was the '80s'. We almost got this one right. These creatures were the correct Ohmy size, but had excessively large brains in their posteriors, causing them to fall over backwards. We sent these off to Nowhereland also.

Let's get back to our current genetic modification processes. I'm sure you've been to our grocery stores to buy produce. Have you noticed how beautiful our vegetables are? Bright green lettuce? Shiny red tomatoes? They look that way because of our genetic changes. They ship well too. They keep their color for as long as one week!"

Clarence jumped in. "I don't think Harry has been to any of our grocery stores yet. What you say is true, Carla, but while the genetic changes have created better-looking produce, they have also taken away any semblance of taste. They are bland and boring. Not only that, the seeds from these plants are used over and over again in all of Baa. All of our produce everywhere is now tasteless!"

Carla became defensive. "But, Clarence, they are disease resistant. I'm sure you'll agree that they taste just fine if smothered by any of the many sauces and dressings now available. If I may continue?

Let's talk about insecticides. Our 'Insecticide Division' is our most profitable one. We produce over two hundred types of insecticides, at least one for every major insect species. Our latest line of insecticides, just being brought to market, kills most insects instantly AND tastes good too! Our luncheon salads today have all been sprayed with one of these products. You'll see for yourself how good it tastes."

"But is there no danger of bodily harm if this product is ingested?" I queried. "What laboratory testing has been done?"

"Our government does testing for us on the jabber population. We are awaiting their results. None of them have died, so it's quite safe, I'm sure.

I'd like to get into my favorite segment of the business: beauty and beauty products. We'll be visiting the Avan Beauty Division, right after our lunch."

With that signal, a food cart was wheeled into the room. There were cans of grassade for each of us, as well as three large trays of food: one with all sorts of greens, another with slices of cured jabber meat and the third with varieties of bread (sliced).

Carla invited us to partake. "Help yourselves, please. The salad greens have been sprayed with our flavorful insecticide, and the jabber meat is from Hormal."

I wanted no part of the greens and was not very excited about Hormal-processed meat, so I filled up on bread and grassade. Hopefully, that would tide me over until dinner.

Carla had some questions as we ate. "What do you think of what we've discussed so far? Is there any interest in the disposal of nuclear waste or genetic modifications? How about our line of insecticides?"

I conferred briefly with Clarence then gave my response. "You know, Carla, that we already have a good handle on nuclear waste removal. We also have concerns about genetic modifications getting further out of control on our planet. As it relates to insecticides, I'm certain that our bugs are different than your bugs. I'm not too hopeful of a good business fit so far."

"Well then," smiled Carla, "Perhaps it's good that I saved the best for last. Let's tour our beauty division."

Carla led us to a large building across the Wow campus. It was simply marked "Avan Beauty Products". She led us inside.

"Here is where the good stuff happens," said Carla proudly. "Perfumes, makeup, jewelry, and accessories. We even have a successful line of silicone udder implants!"

With that, Carla pulled her blouse over her head to reveal what any Ohmy would call "a beautiful set of udders". "Look at these! These are 50% silicone and you'd never know it. I had this done six months ago."

As Carla brought her blouse back to its normal position, I made a decision not to comment. Anything I might have said would have been misconstrued! I just smiled.

"When these were first invented five years ago, we had a little problem with festering sores. Since then, we've improved the silicone compound and it's perfectly safe. Let's see what else Avan has to offer..."

Carla walked us through the facility. We could see them making lipsticks and makeup. We looked at their jewelry assembly line and went to a showroom full of accessories. Carla was now ready to close the deal.

"You've got to love it, right Harry? We have the most lucrative sales model for our beauty products. If you buy into one of our franchises, you automatically get a pink Trigo in which to drive around. You get 30% commission on all the beauty products you sell AND if you sign up others as franchisees, you get 5% of their sales. You'd be rich in no time!

How about signing up right now? We'll start work on your pink Trigo right away."

I didn't think ewe lipstick or makeup would work well with humans. The udder implants would not fit and were made of silicone, known already to create health issues. The jewelry and accessories? Perhaps. I told Carla that the jewelry and accessories were a distinct possibility and that I'd return to Baa in the not too distant future with a beauty advisor. I told her that Eweish jewelry might actually appeal to some Earthlings. We'd give it a try. Perhaps I'd even sign up for my own pink Trigo.

Chapter 24: General Trigo

I still thought about Carla's offer of a pink Trigo as Sheepla took us to General Trigo, the largest Trigo manufacturer on all of Baa.

"Today's format will be different," advised Sheepla. "Percy.81.00.096578 is the Director of Alien Relations; he will take us on a series of test drives in their best-selling Trigos. After you've been driven about, he'll ask you which vehicles, if any, might by suitable for Earthlings."

I thought that this was truly a novel idea. Further, I was impressed that General Trigo actually had someone in charge of alien relations. I had never heard of such a thing, even back on Earth.

As we stood outside in the back of GT's headquarters, I marveled at the long line of test vehicles, presumably organized just for my benefit. Percy gave our party a brief introduction: "General Trigo used to be in the business in selling large, powerful Trigos. They were highly profitable and extremely popular. Fierce competition developed on other planets, however, and we recently found ourselves in financial difficulties; the governments of Baa actually needed to provide bailout funding for us to stay afloat. The good news is that we've restructured our product line, shed some of the poorly performing vehicle lines, and paid back almost all of the government's loans.

We've tried to be responsive to differing target markets. As you are now aware, we have a number of different gene pools here on Baa. Our revised strategy, therefore, is to have a specific Trigo model targeted for each gene pool. We have the "Humble" for the Blacknecks, the "GT Trek" for the Rednecks, the "Baaick" for the Ohmys and Lumens, the "Shevvy" for the '33s', the "Shlepper" for the '00's, the "Ohpra" for the Mouthies, the "Flatubaa" for the Knowbies, and the "Cudillac" for the Bigbeards. We have no specific vehicle for The Technobirds; they want to figure it out for themselves. And, of course, we have nothing for the '51s', as the poor things have no arms.

All of these vehicles are lined up before you, Harry. Where would you like to start?"

I suggested a "Humble" beginning, as the "Humble" best suited my personality. The "Humble" was a small black two-seater. As Clarence and I climbed into this very cramped Trigo, one thing I did notice was that there was ample room on the dashboard for a wide range of religious paraphernalia. There was no air conditioning. There were no power-anythings – just two seats, a brake pedal, a gas pedal, and a steering wheel. As we drove three times around the GT track, I was keenly aware of an almost violently bumpy ride. When I inquired about the level of discomfort, Percy confessed that the bumps were actually in the Trigo's design. The shock absorbers were severed in several places to create the image of humility that the Blacknecks demanded. I complimented Percy on GT's creativity but advised that we'd best skip this vehicle and proceed to the next one: the Baaick.

There were two sizes of Baaicks available: the "Super" for the (larger) Ohmys and the "Special" for the (smaller) Lumens. Percy suggested the "Super" and elected to drive. If I had to choose two words to describe this Trigo, they would be "slow" and "ostentatious". The Super Baaick was designed to be both economical and showy. It was sleek, had three vent holes on either side of the hood, and seated six full-sized Ohmys. The lethargic performance of this Trigo was due to this: To achieve optimal fuel consumption, there was a small methane-powered engine supplemented by "hoof-power". The floor areas next to the driver and each passenger opened up allowing the occupants to drop their legs through the openings and supply supplemental power by "pedaling" the Trigo along. Again, very creative but not for Earthlings. My feet were tired from helping to pedal the Baaick around the track!

Going from pretentious to luxurious, we transitioned from Baaick to Cudillac. Lingo wanted his chance to take the driver's seat, so I sat next to him while Clarence sat alone in the spacious rear seat. The Cudillac was truly "the lap of luxury"; it had power and elegance and was well suited for the Bigbeard politicians. As Lingo roared the Cudillac around the track, he pointed out that the back seat could be isolated from the front seat by pulling a lever that raised a solid black sheet of glass as a separator. The seat in the back also reclined into the trunk space, permitting the occupants to sleep or do whatever. When I asked Percy about the cost of this fine machine, he said that Earthlings could never afford it. It was just a "tease", I guess.

Percy must have been suspecting that Earthlings were environmentally conscious, so he recommended that we try out the Flatubaa, designed specifically for the Knowbies. It seemed like an ordinary Trigo: Two seats in front, three in the rear. There were long tubes connected to each of the five seats. Percy was happy that we asked about the contraption. "While the Flatubaa normally runs on methane, it can also run on methane as supplemented by discrete gas secretions while driving. One end of each tube goes into the passenger's rectum while the other end goes into the methane gas tank."

Clarence drove, Lingo and I sat in the back. We each connected the tubes as instructed; the connection was very uncomfortable. The Flatubaa's ride was bumpy and I felt a stabbing pain in my rear with each bump. One particularly large bump resulted in Lingo's tube jarring loose, filling the Trigo's interior with a foul, putrid odor. We did one lap and returned.

Four more to go. Percy walked us over to the Ohpra; he reminded us that it was a special-purpose Trigo designed just for the media mogul Mouthies. It was my turn to drive, with Lingo and Clarence as passengers.

Let me describe the Ohpra. At first glance, it was just like any other Trigo. When you got inside, however, it became a well-equipped media room with wireless communications (Baatooth), and Holovision receivers and transmitters. There was, in fact, almost no room for the two passengers. As we were not trained on the use of the equipment, it was just a cramped Trigo as far as we were concerned. We did our customary three laps and returned. The Ohpra was interesting but not applicable for Earth because of the vast difference in communications protocols.

Percy walked us over to the GT Trek. Designed for the Rednecks, this Trigo was a dull khaki-colored truck-like thing. A driver and one passenger could sit in front. Behind the front cabin was a large open compartment with two-gun racks and a built-in Haykick cooler. A working ray gun was mounted on the hood. The wheels were oversized and seemed suited for driving in rough terrain. In the passenger cabin were two cup holders and a hose going out to the compartment in the rear. Percy said that the hose connected to the cooler so that you could pour glasses of Haykick as you drove. I told Percy that, if he didn't mind, we'd pass on this one.

The Shlepper next caught my attention. Created for the "00s" and their families, it was comparable to Earth's primitive SUVs. Lingo drove; I sat next to him in the front seat and Clarence took one of the rear seats (there were two rows). As Lingo did the customary three laps, Clarence spent time playing loud electronic games, as each rear seat was equipped with a game console. The noise coming from just the one game console was so annoying that Lingo asked Clarence to kindly stop and pay attention to the drive! I gave Percy a "thumbs down" on this one.

Last but not least was the Shevvy, the Trigo for the "working sect 33s". I was finally hopeful that this last model would be appropriate for my Earthling friends. Clarence drove, Lingo in the front passenger seat, while I lounged in one of the three comfortable rear seats. The ride was smooth and unremarkable. If the cost was reasonable and it ran on natural gas (which it should have), we might actually strike a deal for this model.

Just as we neared the parking lot with the lineup of GT Trigos, sparks flew out of the dashboard and the car started to fill with smoke. Clarence applied the brakes and we made a quick exit, running as fast as we could to our host.

We were lucky to be in a test track environment. Just think of what might have happened if we were out on the open road! A fire-Trigo pulled alongside the abandoned Shevvy, doused it with water, and left it as a smoldering hulk. Percy was nonchalant. "There is no need to wrap our rears about this. We knew about this problem. It's a simple fix and we are planning a recall."

Lingo explained "wrap your rears about this" – it meant to study it intensely. Strange idioms!

However, once again I came up empty.

Chapter 25: Gasson Energy and Rambell Soups

The next morning Sheepla actually came to the hotel early to join us for breakfast. She mentioned that today's two visits were the last ones planned and she wanted to know our suggested next steps.

We said that we'd need a day or two to review our notes and prepare our recommendations. After all, we had made so many visits in such a short time that everything was beginning to blur. Sheepla was good with that suggestion, so we piled into her Trigo again and headed to Gasson Energy's headquarters – our first stop.

The driveway leading up to Gasson Energy's main complex seemed to go on forever. Finally, at long last, a colossal black building loomed in the distance. We parked in the "Visitors" area and went straight up to the Board Room for our meeting. While we waited for our host to introduce himself or herself, I made careful note of their motto, inscribed on a large banner above the white board: "You've got waste? We've got gas!" I was amused...

After a short pause, we were introduced to Maxwell.81.00.019543, Gasson Energy's CEO. He gave us a quick overview of the energy sources on Baa and Gasson Energy's role in the production of that energy...

"Gasson Energy is all about energy, not just methane but a variety of energy sources. We are the largest enterprise in Baa, and we are highly profitable. As the demand for energy continues to grow, we raise our prices to bolster our profits and to plow back money into our Research Division. We are always, therefore, improving our efficiency and seeking new sources of energy.

You may have heard reports criticizing our profit picture and stating that we are 'gouging' our customers who have no other place to which to turn. To that, we say that we are simply applying the simple laws of supply and demand. We have our shareholders' interests at heart, first and foremost.

As you may know, Baa's sources of energy are primarily fossil fuel based. At one time we produced petroleum for our vehicles, but that energy source dried up, so to speak, several decades ago. When that happened, we quickly switched over to methane. We are an agricultural society to a great extent. We have vast areas of crops, and many many jabber farms. All of this produces waste and all that waste produces gas, methane gas – hence the motto you see over the white board.

Before I go any further, Harry, please let me know your sources of energy on Planet Earth. What do you have now? How has that changed over time? How is your waste processed? Only after I know the answers to those questions can we have a substantive discussion about your energy requirements and how Gasson Energy might be able to help you."

I acknowledged that Maxwell had a good point, so I asked for a few minutes to prepare my response...

"The energy sources on my planet were fossil-based for many years. We then developed nuclear power, solar power, hydrogen, wind, and natural gas as alternative sources. Our problem was not so much the limited supply of petroleum but rather the rapid rise in carbon dioxide levels in the atmosphere; we called this 'The Greenhouse Effect'. With the rise in carbon dioxide came the warming of the climate, the melting of our polar ice caps, and an alarming rise in the sea levels. We finally curtailed our petroleum production and now rely on the other, less harmful, energy sources.

How we deal with our waste is yet another story, and not a good one. Our (human) waste goes through a drainage system, crudely 'processed' in waste facilities, and dumped somewhere. Animal waste and farm waste is sometimes used for fertilizer but, more often than not, discarded. Industrial waste is dumped in rivers illegally or 'purified' somehow and discarded. We do not, therefore, make good use out of our waste.

I should ask you then, how do you solve this waste problem on Baa? Do you have any environmental issues regarding your energy production? Finally, how do you propose helping us?"

Maxwell was well prepared. "To efficiently produce methane, you must control the processes at both ends, so to speak. The waste from the Baaners, Technobirds, and Ohmys is all collected and shipped to our processing facility on Baarain. Likewise, the industrial waste from Corporus and the farm waste from the Baaners.

On the Isle of Baarain, we deploy our proprietary production processes to produce methane for shipment all over Baa.

Have we had environment issues? Of course! We have made incremental improvements over the years and now pride ourselves in being the most environmentally conscious entity on all of Corporus. We are all flock players here."

Lingo handed me a note: "Flock players = community minded". I looked over at a smiling Clarence and then interrupted Maxwell. "And what about the Greenhouse Effect? Does your methane consumption does not contribute to global warming?"

"First of all, there has been no satisfactory study to prove whether our rising temperatures are due to methane or due to normal climate fluctuations. Secondly, methane's lifetime in the atmosphere is much shorter than carbon dioxide, your problem back on Earth. I see this as a non-issue."

I thought they were fooling themselves since pound for pound, the comparative impact of methane on climate change is over twenty times greater than carbon dioxide over a one hundred-year period. I continued... "Then tell me, have you had any waste spillage and consequences of that spillage?"

Maxwell, ever confident, mouthed another quick response: "Several years ago, we had a massive waste spill. A large tanker carrying Baaner waste crashed into a bridge in Baarain. All of the cargo dumped into the sea nearby and the wildlife was severely impacted. To appease the residents of Baarain, we paid a penalty of three billion chips and docked a week's pay from the captain of the tanker. Confidentially, we did not think all of this necessary as no Baarain residents were ever directly affected."

"Then please tell me about your alternative energy research. You mentioned that a percentage of your research goes into this category. What is that percentage and have the governments contributed to that research?"

Maxwell grimaced this time. "I'm not at liberty to disclose that percentage and, quite frankly, I do not remember the number. Governments attempted to provide funding in this area but that funding never materialized."

I thought to myself "that's because your lobby pays 60% of their salaries. I get it now..."

Maxwell, running out of patience with me, asked me again "How may we help you, then, Harry? Would you like to visit our facilities in Baarain? Please let me know."

Politely, I declined the Baarain visit, explaining that our busy schedule would not permit it. I also told Maxwell that it would be impossible to manage the waste outputs on our entire planet and that his closed-loop process would probably never work.

We thanked Maxwell for sparing us a few moments of his precious time and we left for our next call.

****

We hustled over to a late lunch meeting at Rambell Soups, knowing in advance that we'd be sampling many of their products as part of their presentation. Their Corporate Hostess, BettyCrockpot.81.00.008753, greeted us. She obviously had a good sense of humor; she was dressed as a red and white soup can with "M'm good" across her udders. She escorted us to a private room within their main dining room. "M'm Good" was posted on the door.

As we were seated, BettyCrockpot started her presentation. "Rambell welcomes the ambassador from Earth and his colleagues. We are going to tell you a little bit about Rambell and its products, then let our foods do the talking for us. We know that you're hungry, so I'll make my introduction brief.

'Rambell Soups', to start, is just a misnomer. The name represents our set of initial products: delicious soups. We have since branched out into many other areas. We have our Sauce Division, our 'Simple Foods Division', our Health Beverage Division, and our Baked Snacks Division. Today, if your stomach will permit it, you'll be sampling morsels from each division.

To start, here is a pitcher of G8, our most popular health beverage. G8 is a tasty blend of eight different kinds of grass. Please help yourselves."

I sampled the G8 and found it fairly tasty, albeit a bit salty. BettyCrockpot continued... "There are different varieties of G8. Some are mixed with fruit; some are tailored to Baaners and some to Ohmys. Some even mix G8 with Haykick to form a delicious mixed drink."

(I gagged)

"For our first course, here are some bowls of baked snacks. Please nibble on some of these for a while. There will be a quiz later," said a smiling BettyCrockpot.

Our server came out with a tray containing three bowls of bright orange snacks. They were labeled, respectively: "Goldjab", "Goldjab Wheat", and "Goldjab Soy Cheese". Each tiny Goldjab was roughly formed in the shape of a jabber. "Cute," I thought, "but they sure are salty." I started some notes on one of the pads provided to us. We made polite conversation while we awaited the next course, which came with a speech:

"For our next course, we'll be sampling products from our flagship Soup Division. Soup lovers across Baa consume more than ten billion bowls of soup each year. Our three most popular varieties are Jabber Noodle, Soy Cheese, and Cream of Grasses. These are among the top ten food items sold in grocery stores every week.

Rambell is also known for its popular, ready-to-serve varieties. We have our Dumpy line of soups, enriched with clods of soil, and our Healthy Harvest soups that have high-quality ingredients, proprietary stocks, no artificial flavors, and no MSG.

Rambell offers ninety soups across our soup portfolio that have been reduced in sodium, and our complete line of Super Healthy soups meet all criteria for healthy foods, such as: being sometimes monitored for fat, saturated fat, and cholesterol, and containing a positive nutrient, like vitamin A.

With that grand introduction and with no further ado, let me bring out sample bowls of our best sellers: Jabber Noodle, Dumpy Soy Cheese and Healthy Harvest Cream of Grasses."

And so, we were served. I took the time to savor a bit of each bowl. The Jabber Noodle was salty and was mostly noodle with just one small lump of jabbermeat. The Dumpy Soy Cheese was not to my liking, as I had no desire to bite into the clods of soil embedded in the cheesy stock. The Cream of Grasses was actually the best, so I asked BettyCrockpot, "I enjoyed the Cream of Grasses. What other cream soups do you offer?"

"A long list, Harry. Let me see what I can remember: Cream of Fescue, Cream of Soybean, Cream of Peanut, Cream of Alfalfa, and Cream of Red Clover. The last one is my favorite."

"That's most impressive. Who does your product taste-testing?"

"I'm glad you asked, Harry. All Rambell employees are given new products to take home and test. We eat our own grasses."

(A note from Lingo: "She means we actually try our own foods first.")

"Ready for your last course? We thought we'd wind up with pasta and sauces. These canned products really help to complete the meal. We have our "Chef Baa-ardee" pasta with sauce and "Noodle-o's" for our lambs. The kinds of pasta are made from enriched grass flour and the sauces from peanuts. Here are bowls of "Chef Baa-ardee" pasta with peanut sauce, right out of the can."

I tried the pasta offering, again finding it salty and artificial-tasting. Rather than wasting BettyCrockpot's time, I thought it best to ask a few blunt questions. "Speaking for Clarence, Lingo, and Sheepla, I thank you very much for your hospitality and your product education. I found the samples rather salty, perhaps containing too much sodium. I'm sure that your products are well suited for the inhabitants of Baa, but I question if they'd work well at home. Would you be willing to travel to Earth to set up facilities there? You could then use your culinary expertise to tailor a comparable suite of products suited to our Earthly tastes?"

I saw our hostess pace around the room. "We are stretched quite thin on Baa. We just don't have enough hoofs on the ground to set up facilities on Earth, I'm afraid."

(Note from Lingo: "Hoofs on the ground means staffing)

As the Rambell staff came around to clean up the dishes, I thought about all of the visits we had made to the enterprises on Corporus. They were in many ways similar to our Earthly corporations. There were similar issues, similar mistakes, and a broad range of inane idioms. We'd now head back to our hotel to recapitulate and make our recommendations for follow-up. To be honest, I had no idea whatsoever on what I'd be doing next. After all, this whole Ohmy tour was just a ruse to learn the Baa cultures and figure out how to settle in as a healer.

Chapter 26: Recapitulation and Distress

After having a less than pleasant luncheon at Rambell, we decided to have one last night on the town before an all-day meeting in Clarence's hotel room the next day. We went back to DuganPark to reconnoiter with Colleen and enjoy some of Baaston's finest foods.

We asked for one of Colleen's tables and, as soon as we were seated, she came over to give us each a big hug. She then rushed out to get two pitchers of Haykick and took our orders. We ordered the day's special: jabber cakes, corn, and baked beans.

There was no mealtime discussion of our long trip. And, not wanting another night at Shears and looking for ideas, we asked Colleen what thoughts she might have for our evening. "Baabaarella," she said. "It's playing in Holovision down the street. JaneFonder is wonderful in it and you'll have a bundle of laughs."

We did go to the show and, yes, it did live up to all expectations. "Baabaarella" was a serio-comedy about an attractive ewe who gets a political assignment to prevent a new "death ray" from getting into the Great Tyrant's hands. There was plenty of action and it all worked extremely well in Holovision. We all felt very much a part of the goings on. Once again, Colleen came through with flying colors.

When I returned to the hotel, there was a large envelope marked "personal and confidential" from SamWoolton. Although I was exhausted, I read the entire document cover to cover, wishing to be well prepared for the big meeting the next day.

****

We had our breakfast in the hotel and started our meeting in Clarence's room. Lingo was there and Sheepla came up from the lobby. I brought with me reams of notes from all of our discussions on Corporus.

Clarence initiated the discussion. "We've expended a great deal of time and effort on this fact-finding mission. I know that there have been some hiccups and some wild fowl chases, but we need to go over each visit one by one to see if something, anything, can evolve into a trade agreement with Earth. Let's make it work, Harry. My congressional reputation depends on it."

(Lingo's note: "wild fowl chase" = waste of time)

I was struck by Clarence's comment about potential damage to his reputation. I really just wanted to travel about Planet Baa to study their society, then come back and set up a shingle as a healer of Baaners or Ohmys. Maybe I should have been more honest and not wasted so much of their time? How could I possibly position the end results of our adventure in a manner that would save face for Clarence? And Lingo? And Sheepla? Was there no good way out of this? I decided to be honest and let the chips fall where they may, so to speak. Hence, my response:

"I agree that we should look at each enterprise visit individually, and I'm prepared to do so. I need to mention, however, that there are such vast differences in our societies and cultures that many of the products and services we have seen are 100% Baa-specific, with no chance of a fit on my planet."

"That may be true, but we need to do some heavy 'out of the pasture' thinking. Let's start with RalphLawn."

(Lingo: "out of the pasture" = creative)

I picked up my notes. "I had previously examined RalphLawn's thick proposal. There are two problems with it: (1) We have quality, competitive fabrics back on Earth and (2) They would give us a license for use of their synthetic fabric modification technology for an upfront cost of one billion chips. I think you will agree with me that their proposal is cost prohibitive. You may read the document if you like."

Clarence shook his head disgustedly. I knew I had his reluctant agreement, so I continued. "Let's look at Baaweiser and Poppyco now. Baaweiser's Haykicks were all bland and tasted the same. Poppyco's products were laden with sweetlah; they would not pass Earth's strict nutritional guidelines.

Then we went to Lazy-Baa. Do you remember that fiasco? Their furniture was all too large for Earthlings."

"But you could seat two or more in one chair," commented Sheepla.

"Not practical; they are not couches.

Now, for Flipped Moss. That was an enjoyable visit and I gave their weedacco product line some serious thought. It would take an act of our congress to get us to even consider importing weedacco. They'd never even allow samples on my shuttle home.

If we think about Baattel, all of their toy offerings were replicas of Baa's inhabitants. Granted, they were cute, but I think Earth's children would have trouble relating to them."

Clarence began to grumble, but I continued. "Sam Woolton's proposal arrived at the hotel last night; I actually stayed up late reading it. Their proposal was restricted to their current set of Baa-specific products – again, little relevance for us.

I thought there might be a market for IBS technology, the robots for instance. If you think about it, the robots were actually crude research prototypes and not ready for 'prime time'. I might consider the robots later when they are productized, but that could take years."

(Clarence began to slump in his chair.)

"Then we went to Hormal. I don't know about you, but I found their products disgusting. They made me sick to my stomach. I'm sorry, but I think I must pass on that one.

The Avan Division of Wow Chemicals did provide some hope. I'd like to ask for some samples of their jewelry and accessories to bring home. I'd do some test marketing and, if the response is good, we might have a viable deal."

Sheepla said that she'd contact Avan to request a set of samples; she'd have them shipped to Clarence's home.

Continuing... "We spent some time test-driving General Trigo's vehicles. They are designed for Baa's paths and roadways and run on methane – two big problems. We have no formalized methane production process on our planet and our road structures are dissimilar. The vehicle that might have had a chance was their Shevvy, but, as you saw vividly, it did not seem safe.

That leaves us with Gasson Energy and Rambell Soups. Gasson Energy focuses mainly on methane production. To get their methane production process to work on Earth, we'd have to have consistent waste management across our entire planet and that's a showstopper, so to speak. Additionally, I did not bring it up at our meeting with Maxwell but methane, over the long term, is much worse than carbon dioxide. More methane might put our fragile planet's atmosphere at risk.

Our last enterprise visit was to Rambell Soups. I just did not like their products, plain and simple. They were too specific to your planet and they all had an artificial taste.

I do not like being the bearer of bad news, but you've heard my summary. The only possibility is with Avan's jewelry and accessories. Clarence?"

Clarence was visibly upset. He paced around the room for a while and glared at me. "This is most distressing. We've spent all this time touring Corporus and the best we came up with is the possibility of trinket sales? I worry about my job!

We are booked on the afternoon ferry to the Baa mainland. Let's adjourn for now. I need to discuss all of this with the House Speaker. I'll see you later, Harry."

And, with that curt note, Clarence ushered us all out of the room as he picked up his Orifice to call Speaker.

****

We did not speak about anything of substance as we boarded the ferry. Clarence refused to even make eye contact with me.

Had I made a huge tactical error in insisting on this tour? What would I do next? Should I briefly visit Leroy and his family, then climb into my PLM and hook up with the shuttle and return home?

Regrettably, Clarence answered these questions as we sat at dinner. "I spoke with the Speaker, Harry. He feels that you have misled us. He feels that you have wasted the time of Sheepla and two valuable congressional resources. You have wasted governmental funds on travel and entertainment. The Speaker wants remuneration. You must pay us two hundred thousand chips as soon as we return or face permanent detention on Nowhereland."

Section IV: Nowhereland

Chapter 27: Help from an Unlikely Source

I could not finish my dinner after Clarence's shocking announcement. I excused myself and started walking toward my cabin. There was no way I could come up with two hundred thousand chips. What were my options? I could try to escape to Leroy's farm, jump in the PLM and hook up with the next shuttle home. That was too risky; I'd never get away with it. If I went to Nowhereland, it was certain death – possibly at the hands of a vicious criminal. Just think: If I had been dishonest and tried to carve out one or two fake trade deals, my life would have been spared. The price for being honest! I was overcome by sadness; I had failed miserably!

I reversed directions and started a long walk to the stern of the ferry. The only way out seemed to be to jump ship; if another vessel picked me up at sea, I had a chance at a rescue. If not, I'd welcome my death by drowning.

And then the miracles started to happen.

Two Blackneck Baaners were resting comfortably in deck chairs watching the sunset and sipping Haykicks. Standing behind each of them was another of the translucent figures I had seen earlier on my voyage. The two strange beings were just standing there, motionless and watching the sunset. I decided to confront the two apparitions; after all, what was I to lose? I first introduced myself to the two Blacknecks...

"Good evening. My name is Harry and I'm an alien from Planet Earth. A beautiful sunset, isn't it?"

The Blackneck on the left looked over. "My name is Peter.76.08.027856 and this is my colleague, Paul.76.08.034679. We are missionaries returning home after some meetings on Corporus. Would you care to sit with us? Please pull up a chair."

As I started to sit in the deck chair next to Peter, I boldly asked to be introduced to their associates standing behind them. Peter turned around, as did Paul. They gave me the strangest looks. Peter spoke first: "There's nobody there, Harry. Have you been drinking?"

I lied. "Yes, Peter. I probably had too many Haykicks with my meal. Please forgive me."

We sat and talked. Paul led the conversation... "We're on our way home after doing missionary work on Corporus. We have a total of three missions operational on Corporus and another fifteen on Nowhereland. Our job is to try to get them to understand the role that the Supreme Being could play in fixing their broken lives. It's difficult work, as you might imagine. Are you a man of faith, Harry?"

"Not really, Paul. I believe that a higher power might exist, but that the connections to that power are not of a personal nature. I sometimes wish I had your faith."

"That's a shame. Are there people of faith on your Planet Earth?"

"Yes, many millions. Those of us with in-depth scientific training tend to lean more towards agnosticism or even atheism. I'm curious, though. Have you had any success on Corporus or on Nowhereland?"

Peter answered this question. "The Ohmys have a problem with greed. It's all about their worship of chips. Some may claim to have faith and actually go to places of worship but, when they return to their homes, they get back into their ruts – make more chips, spend more chips, etc. It's sad. Life should be less about consumption and more about love, friendship, and helping those in need.

Nowhereland is clearly a different story. Many of the inhabitants are desperate and look for salvation and peace. Our fifteen missions are quite active, and we've had a large measure of success. Paul and I are actually off to Nowhereland as soon as we dock. We don't even stop at our monastery for a break."

A polite conversation then ensued. While I found their points of view interesting, I thought them irrelevant.

As I started to say "goodbye", the strangest thing happened; both of the apparitions actually smiled at me and waved!

The cloud of depression overcame me again. I walked to the ferry's stern and looked at the wake of the boat and the gray foam of the sea. The sun had set, and the sea invited me in. As I put one leg over the railing, I felt a comforting hand on my shoulder. Both of the apparitions were standing next to me. And one of them spoke:

"Don't do it, Harry. You have work to do."

"How do you know my name? And who are you anyway?"

"We are angels, Harry. We call ourselves 'Holies'. One of us is assigned to each person of faith. We guide them through their lives, whispering thoughts to them as answers to their prayers. My name is Michael and my colleague's name is Jonah."

I had so many questions! "How is it that I can see you but no one else can?"

"You know about original sin, don't you, Harry? The Baaners were once one with the angels, but they ate from the tree of knowledge (metaphorically) and became disconnected to our realm. We live in another dimension, one shared by all of Baa's inhabitants. They just cannot see us.'

You had the same problem on your planet. Angels are there also, sharing space and time with your humans. Because of the humans' original sin, they also cannot see their angels."

"I think I understand. Because I'm from Earth, I can see the Holies, but the inhabitants of Baa cannot. Wow!"

Jonah finally joined the conversation. "So, our Earthling friend, we have a proposition for you. Please hear us out.

You will be on the ferry to Nowhereland, the same one carrying Peter and Paul. When you arrive on Nowhereland, they will take you over to their mission. There, in that mission, you can set up a healing practice. All four of us will guide you in your new practice. Peter and Paul will get you your patients, while Michael and I will provide spiritual guidance. Keep in mind, my friend, that your healing will be of a spiritual nature. It's not about your making chips."

"If I am not paid, how will I eat? How will I survive?"

"The mission will be your home. There is always plenty to eat."

"And will I ever get home, back to Earth?"

Michael smiled. "That's part of our deal. Mixed in with your 'normally dysfunctional' criminal patients will be the 'top eight' most evil Baaners. You will recognize them immediately, I am sure. If you are successful in healing just four of the eight, we will get you to your PLM for your voyage home."

"Please tell me why you have all of this confidence in me. You've seen my recent failures."

"Because you will add a different dimension to the healing process. Have faith, my friend.

Think of it this way: Brothers Peter and Paul will bring in your patients. You'll do your scientific assessments. At the conclusion of each day, Peter and Paul will pray with you and discuss the final tactical approaches. There are no certainties, but we think we'll be a good team."

And how do I measure success?"

"That's easy. If you see an Holie behind anyone of them, you have succeeded. Do we have a deal? This will be a true test of your skills as a healer."

So, do I jump in the ocean or not? The Holies had faith in me. They would set up my practice on Nowhereland and be there to guide me. Could I trust them? I had so many questions. My patients back on Earth were mostly cases of runaway neuroses; I had never treated anyone who was truly evil. Did I have enough faith in myself? After a surge of newly found confidence, I gave my answer: "Yes!"

I knocked on Clarence's cabin door. I admitted to him that I had no financial resources and that I'd accept my punishment on Nowhereland. I also apologized for wasting his time and wished him well in his future endeavors.

Through all of this, I had learned some painful lessons about truth and honesty, about catering to my bloated ego, and about life lessons that were much greater than I.

When we returned to port, armed guards escorted me to the ferry to Nowhereland. I climbed aboard and found myself in the middle of a sea of undesirables: the scum of Planet Baa. The unsavory vermin included Rednecks, some obviously corrupt Bigbeards, and God knows what else. I was sure that I'd get my taste of all of them while in my missionary capacity.

Chapter 28: Breakfast with Speaker Tramp

It was my first day at sea while in transit to Nowhereland. While trying to savor my meager breakfast, I noticed an imposing Bigbeard sitting alone at the next table. He was tall, like an Ohmy, had straw-colored hair, an orange complexion, and wore what looked like a white golf shirt with grey slacks, together with a "Make Baa Great Again" cap. Perhaps he was one of the "Evil Ones" I was destined to heal? I approached him and started a conversation.

"May I join you, sir? My name is Harry and I'm an alien from the distant planet Earth. You look like you could use some company."

The Bigbeard responded: "I'm Tramp.76.01.000977. You may have heard my name in your travels. I'm quite famous, you know. I really don't like to spend time with anyone other than the Ohmys, but I'll make an exception in your case. Consider yourself lucky."

"Lucky indeed, I've heard your name mentioned a number of times. You were Speaker of the House, right?"

"Yes. I was the best Speaker that Baa ever had! You should have seen the crowd at my inauguration. After accomplishing more than any Speaker before me, I was a victim of a 'Deep State' conspiracy. I was removed from office and banished to this forsaken island."

"So, I heard. How do you plan to cope? What are your plans?" I was hoping to get some information in advance of a potential therapeutic relationship.

"Before I was Speaker, I was a wealthy Ohmy. I built majestic hotels and championship golf resorts. Nowhereland is an opportunity for me to build the biggest and best hotels ever. That's my plan."

"Okay, but how can you finance your building efforts. I did not know that you could bring cash into Nowhereland."

"Have you read *The Art of the Deal*? I'm Baa's most talented deal maker and I've cut a deal for a large plot of free land. I plan to leverage my land holdings to finance the necessary construction work."

I was really curious now. How could he have managed this free land if he was in exile? I had to ask… "How on Baa did you get all of this land?"

"I said I'd build my hotels on top of the nuclear waste disposal area. No problem getting both the permission and the land."

"But who will come to your hotels if there is a danger of becoming radioactive?"

"They will flock to my hotel just because of my name. It's all about brand image, you know."

I saw no point in arguing and decided to change the topic. "Tell me then, for how long were you Speaker? What is your legacy? What were your major achievements?"

Sporting a wide grin, Speaker Tramp quickly responded. "I was the 45th Speaker and the best one ever. I lowered the taxes on Corporus and the Ohmy employment rate was never as good. All of Baa applauded my efforts and I had a 99% approval rating."

All of this did not add up. Baaners don't lie and yet this Ohmy/Bigbeard was saying things that just did not make sense. I pressured him on some points. "You lowered the taxes for the Ohmys. Did you also lower the taxes for the Technobirds and other Baaners?"

"I lowered the taxes for the Technobirds but was quite selective in my tax law adjustments for everyone else. The districts that did not vote for me all had higher taxes, while the districts that voted for me got substantial tax relief. It worked out well."

I was flabbergasted. "Did this not cause an unnatural division in the Baaner population?"

"The division was there already. Those that liked me and those that did not. I just rewarded those that were faithful."

I was amazed. I continued my questioning, this time about Tramp's effort to build a wall around Corporus. "I heard that you built a wall around Corporus to limit immigration. How did that work out for you?"

"It would have been a grand wall, sturdy and impenetrable. The House opposition party fought it unfairly and it was never finished. The threat of an immigrant invasion still exists on Corporus."

"But it's an island. Doesn't its isolation form a natural barrier?"

"It does. But the immigrants could approach by ship, then swim ashore at night. They carry diseases and are dangerous criminals. They are pillagers and rapists. They are bad, very bad.

I was born on Corporus and I am very protective of the Ohmys."

I had to expand my questioning now. "This seems to be both nationalism and protectionism. Why were you so one-sided in your support of the Ohmys? Were you not elected to serve all the Baaner sects?"

Tramp began to get irritated, his orange complexion turning redder with my questioning. "Of course! It's the trickle-down effect, you alien moron. You do things to make the Ohmys successful and then good things happen across all of Baa. Technobirds build more products. Employment levels improve. Even those on Nowhereland reap the benefits. I was elected to serve all of Baa, and I did it well. No Speaker was ever as popular as I. I won my election in a landslide with a great deal of help from my friends on Planet Plutin."

Now I was really curious. "What? You had help from aliens on another planet? I thought you were protective of Baa? How could you possibly do this?'

Tramp was livid. "Listen, jabberhead! Plutinites are my friends. Why shouldn't they help me get elected? My relationship with them was 'perfect.'"

I could not wait to get away from this clown, so I bought one of his "Make Baa Great Again" caps and moved quickly away. I could not and would not consider him a patient for continuing therapy. It was obvious that he had a problem with the truth. Strange, very strange.

****

After three long days, we finally arrived at Hades, the main port on the island of Nowhereland. As I walked down the ramp, Peter and Paul awaited me in their "Humble" Trigo. It was good to be among my new friends as I started on this: my greatest challenge and my greatest adventure.

Chapter 29: Mission #5

Let me describe my new residence, "Mission #5". This, the fifth mission on Nowhereland, was the largest one to be built. There were spartan sleeping quarters in the rear of the building, three small offices, a kitchen, and a chapel seating about one hundred in the front of the building.

I was given one of the three offices. I had a simple desk with a desk chair, a comfortable green jabbercloth armchair, and a matching green sofa. Both pieces of furniture were placed opposite my desk. Peter was kind enough to put a sign over my office door: "Harry the Healer".

On my first "workday", the day after our arrival, I met with Peter and Paul in my office to discuss logistics. There would be no formal appointment schedule; patients would come in on a first come, first served basis, take a number, and wait their turn in the chapel. Every morning we would meet in the chapel for a brief prayer, have breakfast, and then retire to our offices. I was to keep detailed notebooks recording each patient's visit with my diagnosis, notes, and action items. At the end of each day, we would conclude with a prayer and a discussion of the day's events. It sounded easy enough.

****

The next day, my first day with potential patients, was a day filled with apprehension. I started the day with a brief prayer session, held by Peter. We had a simple breakfast, and then all three of us entered the chapel to see what awaited us.

It goes without saying that I did expect criminals from all of the sects. What I did not expect was a number of sadly deformed creatures! There was one female Baaner with two heads, a male "78" with an enormous head, and a female "80" with an excessive large rear end. Including these three pathetic souls, there were three "normal looking" Baaners. The Baaner with two heads, believe it or not, had drawn the "number one", my first patient on Baa. I escorted her into my office.

Her names were Sybil.76.45.064556 and Clara.76.45.064556. As we conversed, it seemed that Sybil was banished to Nowhereland for what she called "a minor crime". She claims that she was caught harvesting grasses from her neighbor's pasture and punished for that crime as well as for resisting arrest. She was sent to Nowhereland seven years ago and camped out with some other ewes in a quiet, secluded area that turned out to be the dumping site for nuclear waste canisters. As was the case with four of her new colleagues, they all started to develop a second head and, along with that head, a competing personality. Sybil was the original (Redneck) Baaner. She seemed normal enough: a bit agitated, perhaps. She acknowledged her early transgressions and ultimately accepted her banishment. As the second head materialized, Sybil sought help from Paul. Clara, the newly formed head, readily accepted Paul's assistance and became a Baaner of faith. Sybil vehemently resisted Clara's religious transformation. With the emergence of Clara and of Clara's newly acquired faith in the Higher Power came exaggerated symptoms of anxiety in both patients: Clara was vocal in her criticism of Sybil's lack of faith and Sybil was angry at Clara's criticism and lack of acceptance. After all, Sybil came first and who was this annoying upstart?

My diagnosis was immediately obvious: "dissociative identity disorder", or multiple personalities. My noted recommendations were continued therapy with an emphasis on developing Clara into the dominant personality. I suspected that Clara would ultimately receive spiritual guidance and, towards that end, from the Holie assigned to her. I prided myself on my diagnosis and recommendation and opened the door for the next patient.

Jimmy.76.00.145358 was a youthful Baaner, just banished one week ago. His crime was grand theft: the stealing of a neighbor's Trigo. Jimmy complained about missing his family and especially his mother, with whom he was very close. Jimmy's case was obviously "separation anxiety". I expected to see many of those cases, particularly among the youth. I reminded Jimmy that he was here for a reason: breaking the "one shall not steal" commandment. My recommendation to him was continued therapy.

Ziggy.78.00.000539 was next. His head was so much out of proportion that he needed Peter's physical support to walk into my office. Rather than being seated, he elected to lie down on the couch. I immediately felt a deep sense of pity for Ziggy, obviously the result of a genetic experiment gone awry. Not surprisingly, Ziggy suffered from depression and frequently entertained suicidal thoughts. I assured him that "bad things happen to good Baaners" and that he should place his trust in the Higher Power. My recommendation was for continued therapy and for spiritual guidance/support through our mission.

Flora.80.00.005767 was next in line Flora was, again, the consequence of badly executed genetic experiments. As was the case with Ziggy, Flora needed physical support, this time in the form of what we would call "a walker". As Flora lay on the couch and started to talk, she reminded me of my old Knowbie friend Betsy. She had Betsy's physical appearance with a posterior (and perhaps her brain) easily twice Betsy's size. I could see why she had trouble walking and retaining her balance.

Flora's case was the most interesting so far. She was extremely intelligent, bordering on "genius". She was angry and agitated. She questioned why she was even there on Nowhereland, a question for which I had no immediate answer. Should I just say, "those were the rules?" Was there any good answer? Why should one so talented not have been recognized as an asset and rather seen as a liability? Did anyone have the right to make those moral decisions?

I told her that everything happens for a reason but wondered, deep in my heart, what that reason could possibly be. As she left the room, I began to question my own nascent faith and whether there really was "a reason for everything" – my own hollow words. I chastised myself for going back to my old therapy methodology. I still needed work on the process of TRUE faith healing.

I recommended continued therapy. Maybe, over time, the true reason for her being on Nowhereland would become apparent. I sure hoped so!

Chapter 30: Caligula

The third patient on my second day was a Bigbeard whose name was Caligula.76.01.009756, the first exiled politician with whom I had the pleasure of meeting.

Here are my notes and some recorded excerpts of my initial conversation with Caligula:

"So, what brought you to Nowhereland?"

"I really do not know why I was exiled. I was Speaker of the House for six months and had many significant accomplishments just in that short amount of time. I was responsible for revising the Baaner tax system, and for many major construction projects. All of my colleagues loved me, and I was revered by my Baaner subjects."

"You must have done something wrong. What reasons were given for your exile? Whether valid or not, there must have been some stated issues."

"Some Bigbeards objected to my building houses of worship."

"That makes no sense. Are you religious? Do you worship the Holies?" (There was no Holie standing next to him; this was a trick question.)

"Goodness no! I built these houses of worship so that my followers could worship me!"

"Do you consider yourself as a god then? Are you related to the Holies?"

"I do consider myself to be a deity. The Holies are figments of a child's imagination. You may bow before me if you like."

I chose to ignore his last sentence and continued my interrogation. "Surely building those temples with taxpayer money must have angered many."

"Yes, but I dealt with them", said Caligula with an evil smile.

"And how, may I ask?"

"Do you know what growlies are?"

"No. I never heard of them."

"Growlies are large, fierce jabber-like beasts. They feed on Baaner flesh. I arranged for a sporting event: my unarmed critics versus a group of hungry growlies. Proceeds from the event went into my temple building fund. It was a huge success."

I gagged upon hearing this. Surely this Baaner was one of "the evil eight" to be converted/transformed. If he considered himself to be a god, how would I ever get him to recognize the Higher Power? Perhaps if I changed the subject, I could get to know him better. "Tell me about your family, Caligula. Do you have brothers and sisters?"

"Yes, I have three lovely sisters: Agrippina, Drusilla, and Livilla. They were all wonderful in bed. I miss my carnal adventures with them."

"Did they have other lovers?"

"Oh, yes. Many Bigbeards actually paid me thousands of chips for their company."

"Did you have these relationships when you were very young, or did they start when you became The Speaker?"

"Good question. I respected their virginity until the time when I was poisoned."

"You were poisoned?"

"Yes. I thought you knew that. Right after I became House Speaker. Someone slipped haylock into my Haykick. I was never the same afterwards."

Now it all began to make sense. Caligula must have been mildly neurotic when he first became The Speaker. Someone was jealous, poisoned him and caused him to slip into insanity. If I could find an antidote, maybe there was hope for me after all. I needed to ask more health-related questions.

"Were you healthy before the poisoning incident?"

"I had seizures from the time I was young. I never learned to swim because I was afraid of having a fit and drowning."

"Hmm. Anything else?"

"I talked to the moon."

This was getting to be more and more a medical problem and not a psychiatric one. As I was a licensed MD, perhaps I could diagnose his many ailments, get him on the road to recovery, and give credit to the Holies. An ambitious goal, but worth trying. If I could only befriend him. I let him ramble on...

"You seem like a likable alien. What are your plans for tonight? Want to toss down a few Haykicks with old Caligula?"

Although highly irregular, and although I frowned on this level of patient-doctor fraternization, I thought it might be to our mutual benefit. "Yes", I said. "Are there any decent places on Nowhereland?"

"It depends on what you call decent! Meet me in front of the chapel after dinner and we'll walk to Eros, my favorite saloon."

****

We met after dinner and followed a winding path to a small shack with a makeshift sign "Eros" over the front door. There was loud laughter emanating from within.

Caligula grabbed my arm. "Come on, Harry. I'll buy you a drink."

We sat down on two adjacent barstools. As I looked around the room, there were Baaners of all sizes and shapes. They were doing unspeakable acts to one another, so terrible that I dare not commit their acts into writing. I was mesmerized by the pulsating mass of ewes and rams. "Disgusting", I thought.

So, this is how Caligula spent his punishment on Nowhereland!

"Pick a ewe, any ewe." Caligula toyed with me. "I dare you."

"Maybe next time. Let's just have a drink for now."

The bartender brought over two pitchers of Haykick and Caligula slapped a pile of chips on the bar.

"Where do you get your money, anyway?" I asked. "I didn't think there was a currency on Nowhereland."

"You have much to learn, my friend. You're talking to Caligula the deity and entrepreneur extraordinaire!"

I decided to just let Caligula drink and talk. He spoke of his family, of intrigues, of familial incest, and of frequent assassinations. This was truly a troubled Baaner from a troubled youth. No wonder he had his issues!

While some healers would look at Caligula's state of mind as a lost cause and chalk him up as "the essence of evil", I saw this sad, broken man as an opportunity to show my aptitude for healing.

We walked back to the mission, arm in arm and singing "Gaudeamus Igitur", a little ditty that he taught me back in Eros.

Chapter 31: Attila and Genghis

The next day, I had my usual breakfast discussion with Peter and Paul. I told them about my previous days' patients and my evening experiences with Caligula. They were happy with my general approach but warned me about getting too close to my patients. They disapproved of my carousing with Caligula but, at the same time, thought it might be a good way to better understand him; it was certainly not how they would go about things! They recommended extreme caution in dealing with the likes of Caligula, advising me that I was under close scrutiny by the Holies and might be assigned a personal Holie if I did good work and stayed focused.

The day started in an unusual manner. Two friends were in the chapel together, having drawn numbers one and two respectively. They told me that they had some business to attend to later in the day and asked me if they could meet with me together, in one session. I told them that this was not possible, that this was a screening session, and that a joint session might be possible in the future. Reluctantly, they agreed, and I started my interviews with Attila.76.01.005213, a Bigbeard politician, of course.

I asked Attila to tell me a little bit about himself: "My name is Attila.76.01.005213. My friends call me Attila the Barbarian, or just plain Attila. I'm here because of my redistricting crimes."

"And what, exactly, are those crimes?"

"I passed legislation to redistrict my congressional area. I did this over and over again until my district encompassed one third of Baa."

"And how did you accomplish this?"

"I created an army to invade the adjacent districts, one by one. I pillaged, looted, and destroyed. I did not think I was breaking any laws because there is no commandment about pillaging."

"But you were stealing their properties, were you not?"

"That's debatable. In many cases I let them keep their homes, just levying burdensome taxes on their properties."

"And were you also guilty of murder?"

"That's debatable too. If I happened to torch their homes and they happened to be inside at the time, some unfortunate deaths may have occurred. I myself did not intentionally murder anyone. Sometimes my soldiers got a little carried away, however. I cannot speak for them.

May I ask why I am here? What are you going to do for me? What is your value proposition anyway?"

I was startled by these questions. "I'm here to bring you peace and tranquility. I'm here to show you how your inner strengths can be redirected to become channels for peace and love."

"But I have peace, Harry. And don't hand me that crap about peace and love. I'm doing just fine here on Nowhereland, pillaging with my friends."

I saw that this was going nowhere quickly, so I changed the direction of the interview. "What if I could bring you unbounded peace and happiness? Look, Attila, you're getting too old for this pillaging stuff. Wouldn't you like to retire to a quiet place in the woods? Maybe start a hunting lodge?"

"Now you're talking, Harry. I never thought about retiring, but it's time I did so. Let's meet again soon."

I saw a light at the end of the tunnel. My initial diagnosis was that he was delusional, not knowing good from evil, and not in touch with reality. With a great deal of effort, he might just come around. We set up an appointment for the next week and I called in my next patient, his friend Genghis.76.01.006439.

****

I was curious about the relationship between Genghis and Attila so, after our introductions, I started asking him questions about his friendship. "I just finished with your friend Attila and, while I cannot discuss the substance of our interview and violate patient-doctor privacy protocols, I'm curious about the relationship between the two of you. Is that something you could share with me?"

Genghis smiled at this opportunity. "Attila and I never actually met in Congress; I followed him by a few years. I had learned of his scheme of redistricting and thought it perfectly legal, so I followed his example.

Sure, I did my share of pillaging and looting along the way, but why not? I had many, many love affairs along the way. Did you know that many of the Baaner offspring are somehow related to me?

Look, Harry. My suspicion has always been that the other members of Congress were jealous and that's why I was exiled.

Once I reached Nowhereland, I looked up Attila and we formed 'Pillagers United', dedicated to the fine art of pillaging and looting. We have a morning meeting right after our sessions with you. Would you like to sit in on one of our meetings?"

"No, thank, you. Pillaging is not my thing." It struck me that there was pure anarchy on Nowhereland. Anyone could do anything they wanted to do in the absence of any legal structure! Caligula could go on partying. Attila, Genghis and other members of Pillagers United could go running around the island, looting to their heart's content. My challenge was to transform these souls who were awash in a sea of chaos. It was much worse than I expected.

I knew that Genghis wanted to go to his meeting, so I tried the same concluding tactics that seemed to work for Attila.

"You're getting some gray wool, Genghis. Aren't you getting a little old for this? Wouldn't you like to find peace of mind, a shack in the woods? A place where you could enjoy your retirement? Maybe do a little farming? I can help you achieve those goals."

Genghis stroked his beard. "Sounds good, Harry. Let me run to my meeting and I'll see you next week.

And so, the two left the mission, arm in arm, to attend the meeting with their pillaging colleagues.

Chapter 32: Berniemadeoff and the Marquis

My practice was doing very well, or so I was just told by Peter and Paul. In this, my first month, I was able to pick up a total of sixty-two new patients: Twenty-five Bigbeards (a high percentage of politicians – no surprise), eight "33s", eight Rednecks, six Ohmys, five Mouthies, three Lumens, two "78s", two "80s", one Technobird, one Knowbie, and one (normal) "00 sect". There were, of course, no Blacknecks. As previously recorded, I had only met with three of the "evil eight" evil ones. Most of my patients had returned for a second visit and quite a few for a third or fourth visit.

All of this led up to today, a memorable occasion. I mentioned earlier that I had been treating three Lumens. One of them, Frank.76.09.084346, had been exiled because of his involvement in the bombing of a shelter for the homeless, armless "51s". Frank said that he was one of the Banners' Religious Right and did not approve of taxpayer money being allocated for sheltering the homeless. He said that he felt sorry for the 51s, but, being a fiscal conservative, the establishment and operation of homeless shelters was a wasteful expenditure. He showed no remorse, even though two of the unfortunate 51s died in the bombing.

In my weeks of treatment, I ignored the taxation / monetary argument that Frank posed and concentrated on the teachings of the Supreme Chieftain and his tenth commandment "to love one another". I explained that there were no conditions attached to this commandment. The 51s were accidents of birth. What if he, Frank, had been born a 51? Would the Higher Power approve of his bombings?

Ultimately, my arguments finally must have sunk in because this day, my special day, Frank came in for his appointment with his personal Holie standing behind him. Frank said that he had been reformed and would spend his remaining days on Nowhereland helping out in the missions. He thanked me for my investment of time and cancelled all of his future appointments.

Then, to make things even better, my own personal Holie finally came on board to help me. She was a relatively young ewe, about five hoofs high with blonde wool and piercing black eyes. She smiled and spoke her first words ever so softly: "My name in Gabriella. I am your personal Holie and will stay by your side helping you as long as you believe in the Higher Power and continue to do His work. You might think my assignment a little bit premature, but you've just made your first successful transformation by your references to the Supreme Chieftain and the Higher Power. Why shouldn't an Holie come over to work with you to reinforce your faith? There's no time like the present!"

We had a grand introductory conversation after which I asked her if she needed anything to eat or drink. Being an Holie, she naturally declined. She'd just hang around and whisper in my ear if I needed advice. Can you believe it?

****

That same afternoon, and after a long break in the action, my fourth evil patient introduced himself. He was an Ohmy, short in stature and nattily dressed in fine jabberwear. We conversed...

"I see that your name is Berniemadeoff.81.00.008434. What brought you to Nowhereland and how may I help you?"

"Thank you, Harry. Several years back, my family and I started an investment company, Madeoff, and Sons. Our value proposition to potential investors was very simple – we'd show an absurdly high return on their investments. We did this by plowing the new investors' cash into the portfolios of the earlier investors. So, anyone looking at the books would see a fantastic rate of return. For this, my family and I were put into exile."

"Let me understand this. You never really invested any money? You just paid the early investors a return based on the flow of new money?"

"That's basically it. It worked well."

"So, what happened when you had no new investors?"

"We had a little cash flow problem, about sixty-five billion chips."

"And what happened to your investors then?"

"They complained a bit. Many of them were high rollers and could afford the loss. There were a few charities that were hurt though."

"And do you feel any remorse?"

"Heavens no. I was able to stash away some money and take it with me when I came here. Life is not unpleasant here, although I miss my friends on Corporus."

"So how do you occupy your time now?"

"I visit the two casinos. Did you know that I own two on Nowhereland? I was able to fund them myself. They're pretty cool actually, a little glitzy."

Gabriella whispered in my right ear. "He's a tough one. Ask him about his philanthropic efforts. Maybe there's an angle there..."

I took her suggestion to heart. "I've heard that you've been heavily involved in charities. Is that true and is there a chance you might help our missions here in Nowhereland?"

Berniemadeoff thought about this and walked about the room. "That's a good possibility, Harry. My casinos are highly profitable, and I do not need much money in this forsaken place anyhow. Let's continue our dialogue in our next appointment. I'd like to meet with Peter and Paul also, to better understand their plans for the mission and see where I could help."

We spent the remainder of our session doing idle chitchat. We talked about his parents and growing up as struggling 33s. We talked about his commitment to wealth, his early successes, his yacht, and his family. Although exaggerated, his Ohmy values were not unlike those I had experienced as a healer back on Earth. Strange, the similarities.

****

I saw three patients after my session with Berniemadeoff. (A joke to myself: Bernie "madeoff" with his customers' money) I was about to pack up for the day when a strange new patient arrived in the chapel. He introduced himself as Marquisdesad.76.01.0123765 and was obviously a Bigbeard politician. Unlike the previous Bigbeards, Marquisdesad actually wore clothing; he was dressed in a striking black jabberleather suit and wore the wool on his head in a ponytail.

I asked Marquisdesad to tell me a little bit about himself. Herein is the initial dialogue:

"I consider myself to be an author of great intellect. I was born a Knowbie in a well-to-do Knowbie family and started my writings at an early age. I then entered politics as a congressional representative. My written works were of such a controversial nature that I was put into exile. That's my short story."

"You have freedom of the press, so why were you punished? What did you write about?"

"You might say that I have a runaway sex drive. I wrote about sexual pleasures. I wrote about my sexual acts and my fantasies. I do not think that a crime, do you?"

"Not really. But tell me more. Was there anything unusual about your sexual adventures and your writings?"

"I don't think so, but that's for you to judge. My latest book, 'Sex Acts with Jabbers' was extremely popular. I wrote about how exciting it was to copulate with jabbers. I had a small herd of jabbers in my pasture and visited them each evening. After a while, they actually lined up at the pasture's gate for their turns."

"Female and male jabbers?"

"Certainly. Males and females equally."

"What about sex with Baaners? Did you have a mate/partner?"

"I did have a lovely ewe as my partner. I had to leave her behind when I went into exile. As far as the answer to your other question is concerned, I most certainly had sex with all Baaners. Male, female, young, old – it did not matter."

"And was there anything unusual about these acts? Anything that deviated from the norm, so to speak?"

"Well, yes. As a prelude to each act, I always wanted some form of a game. The games helped to get me further aroused."

"Games? What kind of games?"

"We played 'crack the whip', 'suck my hoof', 'crawl like a beast', and 'lock me up with handcuffs'. Oh, yes. And my favorite was 'swing from the chandelier'. One of my books was an illustrated guide to all of these games. It was called The Marquis' Guide to Erotica. I brought a copy with me. Would you care to read it?"

"No thank you. I just don't have the time for reading.

I still don't see a valid reason for exile. There must have been more to this. Was there any violence in these so-called games? Was anyone ever injured?"

Marquisdesad frowned. "I'm afraid that there were quite a few injuries. One of my jabbers died of whiplashes and I was arrested for 'cruelty to animals.'"

"Were any Baaners injured?"

"Yes. A few lambs were injured. Their parents wrote up a formal complaint."

A picture was slowly becoming clear. This Knowbie / Bigbeard was a real nonconformist and was probably exiled because he made his congressional colleagues look bad. His adventures and his writings tainted Congress. As I was taking all of this in, Gabriella whispered: "Ask him about his relationship with the church." And so, I did...

"How did the Blacknecks feel about your deviant writings? They must not have been too happy."

"This is true. After they wrote a number of letters of complaint to The Speaker, I wrote a book condemning their criticism. It was called 'Have You Thrown the First Stone'?"

So, here was a ram that knew no boundaries. He alienated his colleagues in Congress and angered the church. No wonder he wound up here! What angle could I possible use to turn him around? I was stumped and changed my line of questioning. "And what have your days been like on Nowhereland? What do you do to occupy your time?"

"I run a sex shop around the corner from this mission. I sell my books, jabberleather clothing, and exotic sex paraphernalia. I do very well, actually."

"And is that how you intend to spend your remaining days? Do you ever fantasize about doing something else? You have a very clever mind and should put it to better use." (I wanted to cater to his inflated ego)

Marquisdesad got out of his chair and walked around, deep in thought. "Maybe, Harry. I always wanted to be a stand-up comic."

This was my angle... "You know that we run a variety show every Monday night at the mission. Would you like to be our next entertainer? You'd need to keep it clean though."

"Do you mean I might actually be accepted by your sponsors, Peter and Paul? After all the negativity I've written about the church and their rigid stance on morality?"

"It's worth a try, Marquisdesad. Do you need a writer for your material?"

"Oh no! There are so many interesting subjects walking around on Nowhereland. A fountain of comic material is just waiting to be tapped. I'll need a little time to prepare, though. How about two weeks from next Monday?"

"I'll check with Paul. He does the schedules. Peter and / or Paul will need to check your outline before you go on stage. Are you alright with that?"

"Well, I guess. I'd certainly like to give this a try."

Gabriella patted me on the head and sported a wide grin. Marquisdesad as a stand-up comic on a Monday night in this very mission. What a hoot! I was most certainly sticking my neck out on this one.

Chapter 33: Hitla and Mooselini

I became so busy that I made a decision to make only monthly journal entries. This is my journal for the second month of my healing practice.

I had quite a measure of success in my second month. I picked up a total of thirty-seven new patients, most of them Bigbeard politicians and, among those, two new evil ones: Hitla and Mooselini. I'll get to those two shortly but let me first give you my progress report.

Fifteen left my practice last month and, of those, eleven had successful transformations; I knew that because they were each given a personal Holie. Four dropped out for various reasons: Personality clashes, illness, etc.

Although I was enjoying my work, bolstered by my successes, I still wanted to get back to my PLM, hookup with the next shuttle, and return home to Earth. The transformation of the evil ones was taking place much more slowly than I had hoped. Caligula was continuing his therapy, although I was frustrated with my lack of progress and not able to figure out the right angle for him. At least he showed an interest and did not drop out of our sessions.

I had better luck with Genghis and Attila. They both showed an interest in retiring from their pillaging habits. What worked with them was my proposal that they have a tag sale at the mission. They would sell all of their loot and place a down payment on a hunting lodge that they would run together. Ten percent of the tag sale proceeds would go to the mission in return for our hosting the event, providing snacks, and doing a Nowhereland tag sale promotion.

Marquisdesad's Comedy Hour was a big hit with the Nowhereland inhabitants; there was standing room only for the second of his two shows. As expected, the first show had a few too many explicit sexual references, so we had a little talk and convinced him to limit his sex humor to double-entendres, which he did extremely well. My hope was that he'd see the value of his humor in lifting the spirits of Nowhereland's sorry lot and drift away from his transgressions.

I saved the best for last: Berniemadeoff met with Peter and Paul and agreed to plow the profits of his two casinos into our mission funds. He quickly saw the value of those contributions: Among other things, we established a Wednesday night soup kitchen that Berniemadeoff actually ran all by himself. And yes, Berniemadeoff was my first evil one conversion success; he was assigned an Holie last week. One down, three to go.

Two new evil ones came into my office last week. The first was a Bigbeard, Hitla.76.01.022264. Hitla was a somber looking Baaner; he sported a short mustache above his beard. It was obvious that he wanted nothing to do with me. Excerpts from my first recorded conversation follow:

"Tell me a little bit about yourself, Hitla. What was it like growing up and what was it that sent you into exile?"

"Ach! I was brought up in the Baavarian Province. My father was a Baavarian bureaucrat; I did not get along with him very well. I went to a Baavarian school at which I learned to sing and participated in the choir. At this early age, I even considered becoming a Blackneck.

My father and I had a falling out later in life. He wanted me to be a bureaucrat just as he was, while I wanted to study art; I thought that I had some skills in that area. The academy did not like my artwork and recommended that I study architecture. I was finally thrown out of the academy and became a homeless derelict.

While moving from shelter to shelter, I became an avid reader of discarded newspapers. Through these readings, I became more and more aware of the superiority of the Baavarians and increasingly angry at the threat of the tides of immigrant '33' workers threatening our economy. These news articles refined my visions for a more perfect Baaner-state.

I spoke in Haykick saloons and gained popularity among my Baavarian colleagues. I spoke of the threat of the 33s. I spoke of better working conditions and a 'pure', utopian Baavaria. It was easy for me to get elected into Congress and raise a powerful local militia. At that point, I had two goals: (1) Exile all the Baaner 33s to Nowhereland and (2) make Baavaria into a 'super state'.

After a losing war with the other Baaner states, I was exiled here to Nowhereland. That's my story."

"I can tell by your voice that you still harbor a great deal of hostility. What have you been doing while in exile?"

"I've been looking for my friend Mooselini.76.01.027757. He was a like-minded Baaner in another Baaner province and is now in exile here. I'd like to find him and go back to my purification process. There are too many impure inhabitants on this island!"

"Like an alien? I take it that you think me impure?"

"Ach. True."

"But maybe I can help you, Hitla. You still consider yourself a good artist, right?"

"Ja. I'm a little rusty, though. I've actually spent a number of evenings painting the Nowhereland sunsets. They are most beautiful, you know."

"Listen to me. I have a plan. I know a couple of talented Knowbie art instructors here on the island. What if I setup evening lessons for you at the mission? Maybe you should consider now that your purification days are over, stop getting frustrated, and pursue your first love. How does that sound?"

Hitla tugged at his mustache. "These Knowbie friends of yours. Are they Eweish?"

"As a matter of fact, they are. You need to get over this business, Hitla. They'll do you a world of good, polish your artistic skills, and bring you the happiness that you've been seeking all these years. What do you say? Come back a week from today. We'll talk again and I'll get you started on the road to your new career."

"Ja. See you then."

And so, it went with Hitla.

****

As luck would have it, two days later I found myself in the company of Mooselini.76.01.035435. I had remembered Hitla's description of his friend and therefore knew that he was the seventh evil one.

Mooselini was the first appointment of the day. He was a bald-headed, tough looking Baaner and made me most ill at ease. Rather than tell Mooselini that I had previously met with his friend Hitla, I decided to save that conversation to the end of our session; I wanted to hear his story first.

He said that he had gone to a Blackneck church school and had been certified as a schoolteacher, something he had neither the time nor inclination to do. He quickly became obsessed with politics, at first enamored by a political movement to bolster the power of the "33s" (workers). He then started reading about the politics in Baavaria and "flip-flopped" his political thinking. He justified his change of heart by stating that what he really wanted to do is improve the governmental functioning of his state.

As he became more involved in politics, he befriended some of the local Mouthies and leveraged the media to disseminate his propaganda and further his cause. He became a congressional representative and a political force to be reckoned with. He went as far as to take some "33s" as hostages to force some local issues in his direction.

At that point in his political career, Mooselini decided that the best way to improve the quality of life in his state was to expand the state's territory by force of arms and by redistricting. He teamed up with Hitla, joined his movement, and ultimately was deposed and put into exile.

All of this led up to the point in my conversation where I asked him about his faith in the Higher Power.

"So, you went to a Blackneck academy for your schooling. How strong is your faith now that you've been through all of this?"

"No proof. No faith. No Higher Power. I believe in the power of the individual Baaner. I believe in the survival of the fittest."

"What if I could show you proof of the Higher Power? What would you do then?"

"Bah. You could never prove it. You're an alien anyway. You don't even belong here on Baa."

I was taken aback by Mooselini's surliness. He was going to be a difficult challenge indeed. Gabriella whispered in my ear: "I think I can be that statement of proof for you. Let's wait for the right time."

Given this show of Holie's support, I regained my composure and ignored Mooselini's insult; I continued my questioning. "So, you believe that you are always in control of your own destiny? That Baa and all of its inhabitants just came about by accident?"

"Yes. What happened at the beginning of time is not my concern. I live for the here and now and try to make our planet a better place. That's my destiny."

I went on the offensive. "But you're here in exile on Nowhereland with an island full of criminals and misfits. Is that your destiny? Is there nothing better in your future?"

For once, the great Mooselini had no answer. He just stiffened up and stared at me. I continued…

"Your friend Hitla is one of my patients. Whereas I cannot disclose the substance of our conversations, I can assure you that Hitla has a new purpose in life. He will be coming to the mission for art lessons so that he could spend his remaining days on Nowhereland fulfilled as a painter. What do you think of that?"

"You've seen Hitla? Where does he live? How can I find him?"

I had his address, of course, and would not disclose it. I did the next best thing. "I do not know where he lives, but I do now he'll be here at 11:00 next Thursday. Why don't you come here at 12:00, after my session with Hitla has concluded?"

Did I do the right thing? What if the two of them got together and created even more chaos on Nowhereland? What if Mooselini started to undo my shaky transformation of Hitla?

As if she understood my thoughts and fears, Gabriella reassured me. "Don't worry, Harry. I'll guide you through this and make it work. Trust me."

And so, I went back to Mooselini. "You were a trained schoolteacher, right? Would you ever consider going back to teaching? Giving it a try right here on Nowhereland? You're an expert in political theory, so why not teach political science to the locals? We could set up an evening adult education course right here in the mission. It would be better than wandering around aimlessly, aspiring to some vague machinations with Hitla."

For once, Mooselini cracked a smile. "Teaching Political Science? What a great idea! You're not so bad after all, Harry. See you next Thursday at 12:00"

Another pat on the head from Gabriella. I think I handled it pretty well.

Chapter 34: Lizzybaadone

There's so much news in my third monthly report!

I currently have a steady base of about eighty-two patients. As was the case last month, I picked up a small number of new patients while a few went by the wayside. Of those, some dropped off for personal reasons while some others were successful transformations, each with their personal Holie.

As it relates to last month's three new success stories, one was a Bigbeard, one was a Knowbie, and the third was our very own Marquisdesad!

Two new evil ones were among last month's new patients but, before I report on their cases, let me bring you up to date on the status of the previous five.

I rarely get to see Caligula. He pops in every once in a while to share his adventures with me, strictly on a social basis. In truth, I do not have much hope for his salvation.

Attila and Genghis raised enough money for their hunting lodge and had started construction. They were still coming in for weekly meetings but, alas, no successful transformations had yet occurred. I had been successful in changing their pillaging aspirations but not the essence of their characters; I still had work to do.

Berniemadeoff no longer stops in for therapy. When I last spoke with him, he was so enjoying the soup kitchen work that he volunteered to run them full-time, alternating between missions. If only I had the same measure of success with the other evil patients!

That brings me to Marquisdesad. The Marqisdesad Comedy Hour became a syndicated event, in a manner of speaking. He now travels from mission to mission, entertaining people and, as we now charge admission, providing much needed funds to support the operations of the missions. When Marquisdesad came in for his last visit, his own personal Holie accompanied him.

Last month's two new patients: Hitla and Mooselini? Works in progress. I did have the opportunity to get the two former friends together after one of Hitla's sessions and with mixed results. They compared notes with each other regarding their exiles and the extent to which they were "unfair". They talked about creating a political party on Nowhereland, one that would adhere to their extreme political views. I told them that it would be a wasted effort as there were too many disparate views among the Nowhereland residents. As they were leaving, they both committed to continuing their therapy. I suspected, however, that they'd soon be off somewhere plotting more tomfoolery. While I was happy that they'd stay in therapy, I was certain that the two of them would be difficult subjects.

So, in three months, I have had only two successful transformations. With just one more evil one to be seen and little visible progress on the other five, my chances of ever leaving Baa seemed remote, if not hopeless. Patience was never one of my virtues, I guess...

****

The last Nowhereland evil one came in today. Unlike the others, she was neither a Bigbeard nor a Knowbie. She was more likely a "00" psychopath, but I'll let you judge for yourself. After she introduced herself as Lizzybaadone.76.00.083459, she talked about her background and the events leading to her exile.

"I came from a well to do family; my father was quite wealthy; he owned a number of jabbercloth mills. We had a large home with a 33 as a housemaid. Dad had chosen a new ewe as his partner and that relationship created a rather unpleasant atmosphere in our home."

"Was it just the three of you in your home?"

"No. My sister lived with us also."

"Were there specific reasons for the tension in your home?"

"Dad was frugal; make that 'cheap'. He never shared his wealth with my sister or me. He treated his new ewe as a queen, however. He bought lavish gifts for her and her family. Did you know that that hussy was carrying on with the maid? Disgusting!"

"There was a great deal of jealousy then. That's understandable. Why were you exiled to Nowhereland then? What did you do?"

"I chopped them up with an axe."

"What? Your father and his ewe?"

"Yes. Into little pieces. There was quite a mess."

"And do you feel any remorse?"

"Not really. I tried to collect on his life insurance, but that effort was unsuccessful."

I turned pale upon hearing this. An axe murderer of all things. Maybe if I changed the subject? "Are you a person of faith, Lizzybaadone?"

"Oh yes! I actually taught Sunday school."

"And how do you reconcile your crime in the eyes of the Higher Power?"

"The Higher Power is all-forgiving. He understood my motives and forgives me."

"Can you be certain of this, considering that you feel no sorrow?"

"Yes. It is written that the Higher Power is a force of love and understanding. Of course, I am forgiven."

This is clearly the thinking of a warped mind. I have no idea how to change her ways. I'll keep probing... "How long have you been here? What has your life in exile been like?"

"I am depressed and lonely. Whenever I tell my story to anyone, they walk away – never to be seen again. I have no friends here."

There might be an angle here after all. "Do you have any hobbies? Any long-term aspirations?"

"Well, I always wanted to be a butcher."

I remembered that there was no butcher currently on Nowhereland. Some residents had taken up jabber farming and processed their own food. (I have no idea how they got the jabbers on the island. Maybe they were smuggled onto the ferry? They breed quickly, those jabbers. Maybe they started with just a male and female and the population grew quickly? Who knows?)

"We could use a butcher shop on the island. What if we set you up in business, with all of the profits going to the mission? What do you think of that?"

Lizzybaadone smiled from wooly ear to wooly ear. "You'd do that for me?"

"Yes. As long as you commit to continued therapy. Let's set up an appointment for next week."

Lizzybaadone as a butcher? Interesting. She might just do a good job.

Chapter 35: The Ohbaamah Strategy

It is now the end of my fourth month on Nowhereland and I've not made any further progress with the evil ones. Very frustrating. Yes, my practice has grown and become successful, but will I ever get out of here?

I've spoken with Gabriella about my frustration and asked for her help. She said that she'd have a surprise for me this afternoon.

****

And she delivered on her promise. At the end of the day's sessions, she introduced me to her leader, President Ohbaamah. I sat at my desk while Gabriella and her president sat in the chairs reserved for patients. President Ohbaamah was in the form of a distinguished looking black ram, graying at the temples. He was translucent like the other Holies but shone much more brightly, perhaps due to his stature within the Holie hierarchy. He spoke first.

"I am very happy to meet you, Harry. Gabriella has spoken highly of you and of your practice. You are to be congratulated.

I know of the deal that was made with you and I know of your desire to leave Baa and return home. I'm here to help you with a few suggestions."

"I'm truly honored to meet you, President Ohbaamah. Thank you for taking some time out of your busy schedule. I cannot wait to hear what you have to say."

"You are most welcome, Harry.

As you most likely know, there is evil throughout the universe and what you Earthlings call 'angels' are just part of an army involving the Holies here on Baa with comparable forces on other inhabited planets. We are strong and we are committed, but we are a limited resource. We cannot be present on every planet and involved in every situation where evil rears its ugly head. We just do not have enough hoofs on the ground, as it were.

Given that, we try to leverage resources to extend our reach. That's why we approached you, Harry. That's why we put together our arrangement. You have done an admirable job in the four months of your practice.

Obviously, we'd like to have you stay here forever but, if you are frustrated and upset, you cannot be an effective healer. So, let's do something to accelerate your progress.

Before I give you some ideas, however, please bring me up to date on the status of all of your patients."

I pulled my notebook out from one of the desk drawers and referred to my notes.

"I have two sets of notes, one set for the eight evil ones and the other for the total set of patients. I'll go over the total numbers first; please correct me if my counts are off.

Since the start of my practice four months ago, I have seen at total of 143 patients. Of those, 92 continue to see me and 51 have left the practice. Of those 51, I think 23 were successful conversions/ transformations. Does that sound correct?"

Gabriella responded to that question. "No, Harry. You actually had 26 transformations in four months. I've been keeping track."

"Good! Thank you, Gabriella. Let me now go into my notes on the status of the evil eight. That's where I most need some help, as you know.

My first of the eight was Caligula. I'm not too hopeful about doing anything for him. I see him socially from time to time, but he has no interest in therapy. It's too bad because he is borderline psychotic and could use the help."

The President piped in, "He is the result of inbreeding among the Caesars, did you know that? His family tree had far too few branches, so to speak."

"I did not know that. That is useful information but irrelevant if he refuses treatment.

I next met with Attila and Genghis. I see the two of them fairly regularly, but I cannot, in truth, speak of any progress. They still refer to their pillaging and looting days as 'the good old days' and I'm fearful that they might be tempted to regress to that negative behavior. On the other hand, they have started construction on a hunting lodge that they own jointly. They dream longingly of retiring there. I'm cautiously optimistic. Maybe, with just the right push, we can have them as two more transformations."

President Ohbaamah smiled. He had something up his sleeve.

I continued... "You know about Berniemadeoff. He was our first conversion and is doing wonderful charity work all over Nowhereland."

"Yes, Harry. Good job. You could bring him back in to help out if needed, couldn't you?"

"Yes, absolutely" (What was he thinking?) "And then there's Marquisdesad. He was my second conversion. I enjoyed working with him; he's very entertaining you know."

"I've heard all about his Comedy Hour. Perhaps I'll have time to see his show in the next few weeks. Good work here also. How about Hitla and Mooselini? Your opinion?"

"I definitely need help with those two. I've seen a few power-hungry Bigbeards before, but these two are in a class by themselves. The only good news is that their attendance has been good and that I've given them thoughts about retirement – Hitla as an artist and Mooselini as a political science teacher."

"Don't worry, Harry. I have a strategy," said a thoughtful President Ohbaamah.

"Very good. My last evil one is Lizzybaadone. She has possibilities, I think. She seemed to like the idea of running a butcher shop for the mission. All well and good, but the trick is to have her repent. To make her feel some sense of remorse for her murders. I should add that I see no future risks with her. Her aggression was directed solely at her father and his partner.

So, President Ohbaamah, that's my summary. What do you think and what is your strategy?"

The president got up from his chair and walked around. "Let me tell you about the process of creation. The Higher Power looks for habitable planets to start the evolutionary processes. With His help, you evolved from the lemurs and the apes. In a like manner, the creatures that are blessed by His intervention on this planet were the sheep. The Baaners, as they call themselves, then did their own genetic experiments to produce the Technobirds and the Ohmys. This experimenting is not something that the Higher Power approves of but, because Baaners ate the fruit of the tree of knowledge, they are free to do that kind of tinkering. What is important is how the end products behave, that is to say, that if a Technobird or Ohmy believes in the Higher Power and follows the commandments, that genetically modified being is assigned an Holie just like any other Baaner. Do you follow me so far? Any questions?"

I was amazed at the President's profound insight. "I think I understand. If what you say is true, however, how come I did not see any Holies among the Technobirds or the Ohmys?"

"Because they do not believe in the Higher Power. The Technobirds are so enamored with their intelligence that they see themselves on a par with the Holies. Their intellect refuses to accept us because we 'defy logic'. It's too bad, too bad.

The Ohmys worship the power of money. They live quarter-to-quarter, obsessed with wealth. We've had very few successes there, Berniemadeoff among them."

"That makes sense. I'm sure the analogs of those situations apply to Planet Earth. Where are you going with this, though? How does this apply to my practice?"

The President presented his punch line. "The Baaners descended from sheep. Sheep are creatures that herd together and believe in herd dynamics. Get all the evil ones together in group sessions and your transformational successes will breed further successes. Trust me on that."

And with that, the president vaporized, hopefully, to be seen again later.

Chapter 36: Group Dynamics

I thought President Ohbaamah's plan was brilliant, but would it work?

Following his instructions, I went about setting up the first group therapy session. It was not easy to coordinate my schedule with their schedules, as I had no secretary to help. Not only did I need to coordinate nine schedules, but I also had to do a fair amount of arm-twisting. Lizzybaadone was shy and reluctant to talk in a group. Mooselini thought it was a waste of his time, etc.

Then there was the issue of where to hold the sessions. My office was far too small, so I asked Peter if I could use the chapel just before evening vespers. He consented, of course.

On the evening of the "grand experiment", I arranged eight chairs in a semicircle in the space just before the altar. I set up my own chair facing the eight chairs and we were ready for the first session.

The evil ones came in one by one and took their seats. Lizzybaadone came first, followed by Caligula who elected to sit next to her. Genghis and Attila arrived together, as did Hitla and Mooselini. The last two to arrive were my converts, Berniemadeoff and Marquisdesad; their Holies accompanied them, of course.

I kicked off the session with a small speech:

"Thank you all for coming to our first group session. As you listen to each other's stories, I think you will each have cause to reflect on the meaning of your remaining days on Nowhereland. I am certain that you will leave these sessions inspired and with a purpose. I promise that I will neither preach nor proselytize. My role will be that of a meeting facilitator, to guide the conversations in a positive direction and to keep us all focused.

I thought we'd start with each of you doing an introduction. Would you kindly stand up, state your name and your reason for exile? Ewes first. Lizzybaadone, if you don't mind?"

Lizzybaadone was obviously reluctant. In a meek voice, she introduced herself. "My name is Lizzybaadone and I was put into exile for killing my father and his ewe with an axe."

The other seven gasped at this admission as Lizzybaadone sat down, much relieved. Berniemadeoff was next. "My name is Berniemadeoff and I was exiled because I swindled large sums of money from my investment clients."

One by one, the others (all Bigbeards) stood up and made their introductions:

"I am Marquisdesad and I was sent here because of my political views. I angered many of my congressional colleagues with my writings."

"I am Hitla and I was put in exile because I did a little too much redistricting."

"My name is Mooselini. I am a friend of Hitla and was punished for the same reason."

"My name is Genghis. I did redistrict as well. Maybe a little pillaging and looting in the process."

"I'm Attila and I had my pillaging days, as did my friend Genghis."

"My name is Caligula. I'm one of the Caesar family and was put into exile because I built churches."

I took control of the session at that point. "What Caligula built were houses of worship, worship of himself as a deity. That's the real reason for his exile.

Enough of that, though. I've gotten to know each of you over the last few months and, at that time, tried to give your lives a new purpose. I have succeeded in a couple of cases and have stimulated thought in other instances. I'm hoping that these group sessions will be just another tool in the process of providing you with a more fulfilling life on Nowhereland.

What I thought I might do is ask Berniemadeoff to discuss his new role in our community. Perhaps it will inspire you. Berniemadeoff, if you do not mind?"

"Not at all, Harry. I don't know if you have been to either of my two Nowhereland casinos: Baawoods and Nowhereland Sun. I set up both of those operations shortly after I arrived here. They were immediately successful enterprises and still are today. The chips started to roll in but, despite this, I felt empty and unfulfilled. I started my therapy sessions with Harry and came to realize that my life would be much more meaningful if I could use my newly found wealth to help those less fortunate than I. So, I started running soup kitchens in the Nowhereland missions. I buy the food, cook the food, and serve the food. Hundreds now come every week and, guess what, my life finally has a purpose. I have a level of contentment that I never had before."

"Thank you, Berniemadeoff. Questions or comments, group?"

An excited murmur ran through the other seven. Mooselini raised his hand. "Good for you, Berniemadeoff. I find your story interesting but irrelevant. We're all lost souls here, doomed to die unhappy deaths. By feeding these souls, you're just prolonging their misery. Let 'em starve and die, I say."

Grumbles in the audience. I thought I'd turn to Marquisdesad next. "I'm sorry you feel that way, Mooselini. Maybe after you hear some more stories you'll feel differently. Marquisdesad, may I call on you to tell your tale?"

"Certainly. Harry and I discussed my childhood and my dreams as a child. I told Harry that I always had wanted to be a standup comic. Harry gave me that opportunity and I now have a syndicated Comedy Hour. You cannot imagine the happiness that I personally get in bringing laughter to those in attendance at my shows. I am truly a changed ram and now have a purposeful life."

Hitla stood up and addressed Marquisdesad. "I also had a childhood dream. I always wanted to be an artist. Harry has arranged free art lessons for me and I'm slowly refining my skills. I find your story inspirational, Marquisdesad. Thank you for sharing your news."

And so, it went on for another half hour. Many questions were directed at Berniemadeoff and Marquisdesad. They were all answered in a professional manner and I had the sense that I had made progress.

Next week, we'd have another session. I just need to be patient.

Chapter 37: Great Revelations

I thought President Ohbaamah's plan was brilliant, but would it work? In this, my monthly report, I'll bring you up to date.

We had three more group sessions since the first one. Everyone was usually in attendance, so that was good. The evil ones were slowly getting to know each other and be more vocal in our sessions. Caligula had taken a romantic interest in Lizzybaadone and I voiced my mild disapproval but to no avail. Hitla was flourishing as an artist; his specialty was floral watercolors and he would bring samples of his art to each group session. He and Mooselini were drifting slowly apart as friends, perhaps because Mooselini was jealous of Hitla's newfound talents or perhaps because Hitla was now totally uninterested in collaborating with him in localized acts of treachery. With each session, Mooselini was becoming a real curmudgeon – more difficult and more cantankerous.

Lizzybaadone set up her butcher shop in a nearby mission. As we had agreed, all of the profits went in support of our missions' operations. She actually was quite adept at slicing up the jabbermeat and presenting the steaks artistically in the shop.

Construction was completed on the hunting lodge owned by Genghis and Attila; they had just started their marketing campaigns to attract customers. They seemed well underway in achieving their retirement goals.

There is no news to report on Berniemadeoff and Marquisdesad, other than their valuable contributions to each and every group session.

So, one month has passed and no new transformations. Given this, I discussed my frustration with Gabriella, asking her if I could once again lean on the skills of President Ohbaamah. She said that he'd be at the next group session and had another plan.

****

It was the evening of the next session. I had previously told each of the evil ones that this was an important session and that they should make every effort to attend. Luckily, I had a full house.

All of the patients were seated in the usual semicircular pattern and in their usual seats (creatures of habit) with one exception – once Hitla arrived, Mooselini decided to move away from him and to the opposite end of the semicircle. It was a deliberate affront.

President Ohbaamah and Gabriella took their positions, standing just in back of me. I was most curious as to what they had in mind.

After the usual beginning protocol, Gabriella whispered in my ear. "Clap your hands, Harry."

I did as she suggested. With the clapping of my hands, Both President Ohbaamah and Gabriella, previously visibly only by me, became immediately visible to the entire group of evil ones!

President Ohbaamah addressed the group. "My name is Ohbaamah and I am the president of Baa's army of Holies. Our job is to help any true believer of the Higher Power with their struggles in their Baaner lives. We are normally invisible to all except Harry. Harry, being an alien and being a believer in the Higher Power, has always been able to see us and converse with us. We became visible to you this evening, at his request. We are here to demonstrate the reality of the Higher Power and to help any true believers in their future journeys. The way it works is this: Once you truly reform and become a believer, a personal Holie is assigned to you to work with you for the remainder of your lives. Any questions?"

With the exception of Mooselini, each and every evil one stared at the two apparitions in amazement. Mooselini stood up and addressed the President. "You were not born here; you are not a Baaner citizen. Moreover, this is just a clever trick. Harry is using Holovision to project these images. Don't you all see this? It's all just one big deception!"

And with that, Mooselini walked out, never to be seen again.

Lizzybaadone was the next to pose a question. "Thank you for your intercession, President Ohbaamah. How do we know that we've been assigned an Holie? How does it work if we have a personal Holie and wish to communicate with him or her?"

President Ohbaamah walked over to Lizzybaadone, gave her a hug, and then spoke: "It is a matter of faith, my child. The way faith works is counter intuitive. First, you believe, and then you connect with the Higher Power through the Holies as your intermediaries. As far as the communication process goes, that's the power of prayer. Pray fervently and frequently and the Holies will ultimately provide some form of the answer. You will know that the answer came to you because the answer will be obvious and usually will be something that defies coincidence."

"I believe", said Lizzybaadone. And with that, her brand new Holie appeared behind her.

President Ohbaamah continued answering questions and, before the session terminated, Hitla had become a believer with his own personal Holie. I had now met my goal of transforming four out of the evil eight and could plan my exit from Baa.

At Gabriella's suggestion, I clapped my hands once again and caused the president and Gabriella to disappear from view.

The session did not end on time. Everyone lingered, buzzing with excitement. They even stayed to attend the evening vespers with Peter and Paul.

Chapter 38: The Crossroad

True to their word, Peter and Paul met with me the next day. They expressed their gratitude and presented me with a set of papers that included a signed pardon, some other Nowhereland release papers, and the Baa Medal of Honor. They arranged for my ferry ticket and a police escort to Leroy's farm. After all of this time on Baa, I was finally ready to shuttle back to Earth. The return ferry was scheduled for the day after tomorrow.

When I told the seven remaining (formerly) evil ones of my pending departure, they banded together and arranged a sendoff party for my last night on Baa. We would first go to the Marquisdesad Comedy Hour, then to "Dregs of Nowhereland", a local Haykick saloon.

****

Marquisdesad was his usual entertaining self, doing his standup routine before a packed audience.

Here is his best joke of the night: "An out-of-towner Baaner was driving his Trigo through a small town and passed a restaurant. He wanted to make a U-turn but saw a police officer just up ahead. He pulled up and asked the officer, 'Excuse me, but can you make a U-turn?' The officer looked at him and said, 'Well hell yeah! I can even make her eyes bug out!'"

After an hour of belly laughs, we all went to the saloon and sat at a large table, one previously reserved for the eight of us. After we ordered our first round of Haykicks, Lizzybaadone stood up and asked all of the saloon's patrons for silence. She trembled nervously for a few seconds, and then picked up a paper with her prepared speech:

"Speaking for all of us, Harry, we want to thank you for your hard work and dedication. Because of you and your undying commitment to us, we all have a new and positive outlook on life. Our lives on Nowhereland now have a true purpose and, for that, we are eternally grateful.

We each have a little gift to give you as a small reward for your efforts. We love you, Harry, and wish you well on your next adventures.

Here is my gift: a jabberbone-handled butcher knife engraved with your name. When you get back home and carve up whatever you fellow Earthlings eat for dinner, please think of me back in my Nowhereland butcher shop."

Tears welled up in my eyes. I did not expect this show of gratitude and love. I was really just doing my job so that I could escape from Baa and go home.

One by one, they came up to me. Hitla gave me a lovely watercolor, a scene with wildflowers and grasses. "I painted this just for you, Harry. Flowers and grasses from the mission #5 garden. Ja, I'll miss you too."

Marquisdesad presented me with an autographed jabberleather whip. "I use one just like this in my show, Harry. It always brings laughter when I crack the whip and cause some poor volunteer from the audience to grovel at my feet. Stay well, Harry. Nowhereland will miss you."

Genghis and Attila brought me a stuffed growlie head that had been slated for a wall in their lodge. Attila spoke for the two of them: "We know you don't have growlies back on Earth, Harry, so we've captured and decapitated one just for you. Don't worry, we'll find another one for our lodge. If you ever return to Baa, please come over and stay at the lodge as our guest."

Berniemadeoff gave me a signed copy of his book "The Ethics of Investing". "You have brought real meaning to our lives, Harry. Every time I dish out a meal at one of the soup kitchens, I think of how you've helped me and helped each one of us. Have a safe trip home."

Last but not least, Caligula brought me a box of multicolored condoms. "These are Baaner-sized, Harry. If they fit, think of me when you use them. If they don't fit, well, you can always use them as wall decor.

Seriously, Harry, this was just a gag gift. Speaking for all of us, we wish you well in whatever you do. I'll miss you and we'll miss you. How about a few words?"

Reluctantly, I stood up: "You have no idea how touched I am by all of this. As you all know, I have spent almost half a year touring your planet. I've spent time with the Baaners, visited the Technobirds, and visited a large number of Ohmy enterprises. When I was punished and exiled to Nowhereland I have to admit that I was anxious and frightened; I did not know what to expect.

I have had many patients in my months here. I've helped quite a few, yourselves included, to realize some purpose in their lives. You know what, though? The seven of you have been, by far, the most rewarding experience. You are very special, and I'll always remember you."

As I finished my last words, Hitla interrupted me. "So, given that Harry, why must you leave?"

I had no answer to that. Maybe, just maybe, I belonged here after all.

Berniemadeoff picked up the ewekelele that he had brought into the saloon. He sang some folksongs as he artfully played his instrument. Lizzybaadone and I got up and danced to the music.

Chapter 39: The Baa Glossary

76. Genetic pool code for Baaners

76.00 Sect code for "normal" Baaners

76.01 Sect code for Baaner Bigbeards

76.02 Sect code for Baaner Mouthies

76.08 Sect code for Baaner Blacknecks

76.09 Sect code for Baaner Lumens

76.11 Sect code for Baaner Knowbies

76.33 Sect code for Baaner lower class

76.45 Sect code for Baaner Rednecks

76.51 Sect code for Baaner "armless"

77. Genetic pool code for Technobirds

78. - 80. Genetic pool codes for genetics gone awry

81. Genetic pool code for Ohmys

Avan: The leading cosmetics enterprise on Baa

Baa: The local name for the planet Cetus-2, a satellite of the star Durre Menthor

Baabee Doll: A popular toy from Baatel

Baaner: A sheep-like inhabitant of Baa

Baarain: An island supplying much of Baa's energy

Baaston: The capital of Corporus

Baatel: Baa's leading toy manufacturer

Baavaria: A Baaner state

Baaweiser: A Haykick producer

Baawoods: A casino

Blacknecks: Baaners with necks stained black (priests)

Bigbeards: Baaner politicians

Chips: The unit of currency on Baa

Corporus: The land of the "corporate giants", the Ohmys

DuganPark: A restaurant in Baaston

Emewe: A large bird on Baa

Eweish: Ewe-like

Ewekelele: A musical instrument

Ewette: A teenage ewe

Fire-Trigo: Fire engine

Gasson Energy: The largest producer of energy on Baa

Grassade: A popular drink, made of grasswater

Grasswater: A Baaner non-alcoholic drink

Growlies: Fierce jabber-like, Baaner eating beasts

Haykick: The Baaner equivalent of beer

Haylock: A deadly poison

Higher Power: The Baaner name for God

Holies: Spiritual beings, worshipped by some Baaners

Holovision: Television with holographic images

Hoofs: A unit of distance on Baa. A little less than "a foot"

Hoops: A Baaner competitive sport

Hoopster: A position player in a game of Hoops

Hormal: A supplier of processed food on Baa

Jabber: An ape-like inhabitant of Baa

Jabbercloth: Cloth made from the hair of jabbers

Jabberleather: Leather made from a jabber's skin

Jabberwear: Clothes made from jabbercloth

Jabberwool: Wool made from the hair of jabbers

Knowbies: The Baaner intelligencia

Lambson: The male son of a Baaner

Lazy-Baa: A Baaner furniture manufacturer

Mouthie: A member of the Baaner media

New Baa Rifle Association: Baa's NRA

Nowhereland Sun: Another casino

Ohmy: A corporate giant

Orifice: The flagship product on Mesa View

Nowhereland: Where criminals are exiled

Pastureton: The center of Baaner government

PLM: Landing module

Poppyco: A beverage producer

Poppycola: Poppyco's flagship beverage

RalphLawn: A producer of clothing and fabrics
Rambell Soups: A producer of soup-related products
Rednecks: Baaners with red necks
Sheepicide: The murder of a Baaner
Technobirds: The technical inhabitants of Baa
Transitioner: A Baaner psychologist / coach
Trigo: The vehicle used by the Baaners
Weedacco: The leaves smoked by Baaners
Weedette: The product containing weedacco
Woolmart: Baa's leading retailer

Chapter 40: Baaography (A Baa Biography)

Attila: A congressman accused of pillaging and looting
Baabaa: A famous talk show host
Berniemadeoff: An Ohmy swindler
BettyCrockpot: A food spokesperson and celebrity
BrookeSpiels: The Lazy-Baa spokesperson
Caligula: A psychotic congressman
Doctor Baz: A health show celebrity
Genghis: A congressman accused of pillaging and looting
Hitla: A congressman guilty of excessive redistricting
JaneFonder: An actress
LadyBaabaa: A pop celebrity and singer
Leonardbernwool: A famous composer and conductor
Lizzybaadone: An axe murderer
Marquisdesad: A political prisoner on Nowhereland
Mooselini: Another congressman guilty of excessive redistricting
Ohbaamah: President of the Holies
SamWoolton: Founder of Woolmart
Tramp: Former Speaker of the House
Trayback: Host of the Wager Show

Chapter 41: Acknowledgements

Many thanks to:

Adam Altson
Bob Lee
Linda Bunker
Nick Morgan
Jack Powell
Ricky Sides

Chapter 42: About the Author

This is John Altson's third novel. *.Luke2,* a Christian novel, was published in 2011. *The Id from Eden*, a sci-fi thriller, was published in 2012.

John has also published three children's books: *What Happened to Grandpa? A child views the hereafter through the world's major religions* was published in 2009, *The A to Z of Forgotten Animals* was published in 2010, and *Veggies, A - Z See 'em, Rhyme 'em, Cook 'em, Eat 'em* was published in 2013.

Prior to his writing career, John Altson spent fifty years in high technology and computers. Among his past achievements have been (1) leading the software effort on the mission planning for the SR-71 spy plane, (2) Introducing automated classified advertising to many major worldwide newspapers, and (3) bringing IBM speech recognition technology out of Watson Laboratory and into *The New York Times*.

John has a degree in mathematics from Hunter College in New York City and is a member of Pi Mu Epsilon, the Mathematics Honor Society. He has been called upon to be a guest lecturer at Harvard University.

Chapter 43: Topics for Discussion:

How did Harry's character change during the course of the book?

Did Harry's faith change? If so, how?

What are the parallels between the House of Congress on Baa and the U.S. Congress in 2014?

How is a congressman paid on Baa? Are the influences of corporate Baa on politics just as pronounced as they are in the U.S.?

Is there a separation of church and state on Baa? Explain.

How are punishments administered on Baa? Is there a death penalty?

What are the rights of females on Baa?

What are the Baaner attitudes on stem cell research and genetic modification?

Explain the roles of the Blacknecks and the Holies.

What are the Baaner gun control issues, if any?

How do the Baaners cope with drug usage?

Generally speaking, is life on Baa better than life on Earth? Why?